“Why extend y

e me?” Clair ask y than full of th s aiming for. “Dic f scooping up the

“He was still alive when I started proceedings and, no, I didn’t get anything near what I wanted. Don’t make out like you’re some kind of prey just because you’re used to being the predator. You get to keep the money,” Aleksy taunted softly.

“No matter what?”

The jerky toss of her head was supposed to convey brash confidence. The question was real, though. She couldn’t help being seduced by the prospect of running the foundation her way, without needing approval on every detail. Without having to reveal that each of those details touched her personally and that was why she was fighting so hard for them.

“I’m not into anything kinky,” she warned. “If you’re looking for someone to spank you, move along to the next girl in the secretarial pool.”

“I’m not the submissive in *any* relationship,” he assured her dryly. “I like straight sex and lots of it. I don’t hurt women—ever—if that’s what you’re dancing around asking. I might play with dominating her, controlling her…”

He flexed his hands on her elbows, making her breasts press into his chest. Excitement returned with a spear of pleasure straight into her loins. She gasped.

“If she likes

Dear Reader,

This story has a history as long and colourful as the country it's set in.

Clair is a heroine I lived with for at least a decade before I properly wrote her story. I knew she was pretending to be mistress to an impotent man—one who was using her to hide his criminal activities—but I had her paired with one wrong hero after another. At one point he was a CIA agent, another time he was a New England playboy. For a while she was an accountant, and in one version she asked the hero for an affair, rather than being acquired as a mistress as she is by Aleksy.

Aleksy, with his scar and his very dark past, is the perfect contrast to the flawless and aloof appearance that disguises Clair's surprisingly sensitive personality. What I love most about Clair is her ability to bring Aleksy back to the man he was meant to become. He, in turn, gives her the promise of the family that she truly deserves.

I hope you find their story as satisfying to read as it was for me to finally write it.

Dani

THE RUSSIAN'S ACQUISITION

BY

DANI COLLINS

Published in Great Britain 2014
by Mills & Boon, an imprint of Harlequin (UK) Limited,
Eton House, 18-24 Paradise Road, Richmond, Surrey, TW9 1SR

ISBN: 978-0-263-90916-6

Harlequin (UK) Limited's policy is to use papers that are natural, renewable and recyclable products and made from wood grown in sustainable forests. The logging and manufacturing processes conform to the legal environmental regulations of the country of origin.

Printed and bound in Spain
by Blackprint CPI, Barcelona

Dani Collins discovered romance novels in high school and immediately wondered how a person trained and qualified for *that* amazing job. She married her high school sweetheart, which was a start, then spent two decades trying to find her fit in the wide world of romance writing, always coming back to Mills & Boon® Modern™ Romance.

Two children later, and with the first entering high school, she placed in Harlequin's *Instant Seduction* contest. It was the beginning of a fabulous journey towards finally getting that dream job.

When she's not in her Fortress of Literature, as her family calls her writing office, she works, chauffeurs children to extra-curricular activities, and gardens with more optimism than skill. Dani can be reached through her website at www.danicollins.com

Recent titles by the same author:

THE ULTIMATE SEDUCTION
(The 21st Century Gentlemen's Club)
A DEBT PAID IN PASSION
MORE THAN A CONVENIENT MARRIAGE
PROOF OF THEIR SIN

To the editorial team in London,
especially Suzy Clarke and Laurie Johnson.

Suzy because she fell for Aleksy early and told me to keep him on the back burner (that's why he smolders), and Laurie because she fell for him as soon as she met him (and then told me how to make him even more brooding and irresistible).

Thanks, ladies!

CHAPTER ONE

I miss waking up with you.

THE NOTE STRUCK a pang of wistfulness in Clair Daniels's chest. She wondered if anyone would ever write something so romantic to her. Then she recalled the waves of emotional highs and lows Abby had been riding for months, all under the influence of that elusive emotion called "love." Being independent was more secure and less hurtful, she reminded herself. And the roller coaster she'd been through in the last two weeks, after losing a man who was merely a friend and mentor, was brutal enough.

Still, she had to hide envy as she handed the note back to Abby and said with a composed smile, "That's very sweet. The wedding is this weekend?"

Abby, the firm's receptionist, nodded with excitement as she placed the card back in the extravagant bouquet Clair had admired. "I was just saying to everyone—" She waved at the ladies gathered with their morning coffee. "I texted him that after Saturday, we can wake up together forev..." She trailed off as it struck her who she was talking to.

The horseshoe of women dropped their gazes.

Clair's throat closed over a helpless *I wasn't waking up with him*. She'd never slept with anyone but couldn't say so. Her confidentiality clause with Victor Van Eych had made such confessions impossible.

Still, she knew everyone had thought her relationship to the boss went deeper than merely being his PA. The gossip had eaten her up, but she'd let it happen out of kindness for a man whose self-assurance had been dented by age. Other people's opinions of her shouldn't matter, she'd told herself. Victor was nice to her. He had encouraged her to start the foundation she'd always dreamed of. Letting a white lie prevail in return had seemed harmless.

Then his family had refused to let her into his mansion to so much as share condolences, turning their backs and pushing her to the fringes like a pariah.

She wasn't someone who wore her heart on her sleeve, but the one person she had begun to count on had *died*. Shock and sorrow had overwhelmed her. Thankfully she'd had a place to bolt to for a week and absorb her loss. Ironic that it had been the orphanage, but what a timely reminder how important the home and foundation were, not just to her, but to children as alone as she was.

Now she was feeling more alone than ever, trying not to squirm under the scrutiny of her colleagues, not wanting to reveal that her chest had gone tight and her throat felt swollen. It wasn't just Victor's unexpected death getting to her, but a kind of despair. Would anyone ever stick? Or was she meant to walk through life in isolation forever?

Into the suffocating moment, the elevator pinged and the doors whispered open. Clair glanced over her shoulder to escape her anxiety, and what she saw made her catch a startled breath.

A hunting party of suits invaded the top floor. It was the only way to describe the tribe of alert, stony-faced men. The last off the elevator, the tallest, was obviously their leader. He was a warrior whose swarthy face wore a blaze of genuine battle injury. At first that was all Clair saw: the slash of a pale scar that began where his dark hair was combed back from his hairline. It bisected his left eyebrow, angled from his cheekbone toward the corner of his mouth, then dropped off his clean-shaven jaw.

He seemed indifferent to it, his energy completely focused on the new territory he was conquering. His armor-gray suit clung with perfect tailoring to his powerful build. With one sweep of his golden-brown eyes, he dispersed the clique of women in a subtle hiss of indrawn breaths and muted clicks of retreating heels.

Clair couldn't move. His marauding air incited panic, but her feet stayed glued to the floor. She lifted her chin, refusing to let him see he intimidated her.

Male interest sparked to life as he held her stare. His gaze drifted like a caress to her mouth, lowered to her open collar and mentally stripped her neatly belted raincoat and low-heeled ankle boots.

Clair set her teeth, hating these moments of objectification as much as any woman, but something strange happened. Her paralysis continued. She wasn't able to turn away in rejection. Heat came to life in her abdomen like a cooling ember blown into a brighter glow. Warmth radiated into her chest and bathed her throat.

His attention came back to her face, decision stamped in his eyes. She was something he would want.

She blushed, still unable to look away. A writhing sensation knotted in her stomach, clenching like a fist when he spoke in a voice like dark chocolate, melting and rich, yet carrying a biting edge.

She didn't understand him.

Clair blinked in surprise, but he didn't switch to English. His command had been for one of his companions, yet she had the impression he'd been talking about her if not to her. He swung away, moving into the interior offices as if he owned the place. One of the men flanking him murmured in a similar language.

"Was that Russian?" Clair asked on a breathless gasp as the last pin-striped back disappeared. She felt as if a tank had just flattened her.

"They've been coming in all week. That tall one is new." Abby dragged her gaze away from the hall and became conspiratorial as she leaned over her keyboard. "No one knows what's going on. I was hoping you could enlighten us."

"I wasn't here," Clair reminded her. She hadn't even been in London. "But Mr. Turner told me before I left that everything would carry on as usual, that the family were keeping things status quo until they'd had time to settle his private affairs. Are they lawyers?" She glanced toward the hall but was certain that man wasn't anything as straitlaced as a lawyer. He struck her as someone who made his own rules rather than living by any imposed on him. Her skin still tingled under the brand of ownership he'd imprinted on her.

"Some are, I think," Abby answered. "Ours have been meeting them every day."

"Our—? Oh, right." Clair forced herself back to the conversation. Lawyers. Not just her friend deceased but the boss and owner, leaving the place on tiptoes of tension. She'd noticed the mood the second she returned. Having strangers prowl like bargain hunters at a fire sale didn't help. Clair decided she didn't like that trespasser of a man.

Abby glanced around before hunching even closer. "Clair? I'm really sorry for what I said. I know losing Mr. Van Eych must be hard for y—"

"It's fine. Don't worry about it," Clair dismissed with a light smile. She stepped back to freeze out the empathy.

Putting up walls was a protective reflex, an automatic reaction that probably accounted for why no one ever sent her flowers or love notes. She wasn't good at being close to people. That was why she'd let herself fall into a fake romance with Victor. He'd offered companionship without the demands of physical or emotional intimacy, protecting her from anyone else trying to make a similar claim. No risk, she'd thought. No chance of pain.

Ha.

That Russian would make incredible demands, she thought, and her stomach dipped even as she wondered where her speculation had come from. No way would she let someone like that into her private life. He was a one-way ticket to a broken heart. Forget him.

Nevertheless, trepidation weakened her knees as she looked toward her office, the direction he'd taken. Silly to be afraid. He would already have forgotten her.

"I'll check in with Mr. Turner," Clair said, holding the smile of confident warmth she'd perfected as Victor's PA. "If I'm able to tell you anything, I will."

"Thank you." Abby's worried brow relaxed.

Clair walked away, determined to push the Russian from her mind, but she'd barely hung her coat and bent to tuck her purse into her desk drawer before Mr. Turner appeared in the doorway. Waxen paleness underpinned the flags of red in his sagging cheeks.

Clair stood to attention, heart sinking with intuitive fear. "What's wrong?"

"You're to report to—" He ran a hand over his thinning hair. "The new owner."

Aleksy Dmitriev set the waste bin next to his feet, reached for the first plaque on the wall and tossed it in, taking less satisfaction in the loud *clunk* of an industry award hitting the trash than he'd anticipated. This coup had been too easy. *Clunk.* The bastard wasn't alive to see his world collapse. *Clunk.* Van Eych had succumbed to the lifestyle he'd enjoyed at the expense of men like Aleksy's father rather than face the revenge Aleksy had intended to wreak. *Clunk.*

The blonde in the foyer was that filthy dog's mistress. *Smash!*

A delicate crystal globe shattered in the bottom of the can, leaving a silver heart exposed and dented.

"What on earth," a clear female voice demanded, "do you think you're doing?"

Aleksy lifted his head and was struck by the same kick of sexual hunger he'd experienced fifteen minutes ago. The part of his anatomy he couldn't control suffered another tight, near-painful pull.

At first sight he'd judged her snowflake perfect, delicate and cool with creamy, unblemished skin, white-gold hair and ice-blue eyes. As potent as chilled vodka with a kick of heat that spread from the inside. He'd demanded her name and details.

Now the dull raincoat was gone, revealing warmer colors. Her peach knit top clung to slender arms and hugged smallish but high breasts, while her hips flared just enough to confirm she was all woman.

He smothered reckless desire with angry disgust. How could she have given all that to an old man, especially *that* old man?

Under his stare, her lashes flickered with uncertainty. She turned one boot in before setting her feet firmly. Her fists knotted at her sides, and her shoulders went back. Her chin came up in the same challenge she'd issued when they first came face-to-face.

"Those might have sentimental value to Mr. Van Eych's family," she said.

Aleksy narrowed his eyes. The heat of finding the fight he'd been anticipating singed through his muscles. She was an extension of Victor Van Eych, and that allowed him to hate her, genuinely hate her. His sneer pulled at his scar. He knew it made him look feral and dangerous. He was that and more. "Close the door."

She hesitated—and it irritated him. When he spoke, people moved. Having a slip of a woman take a moment to think it over, look *him* over, wasn't acceptable.

"As you leave," he commanded with quiet menace. "I'm throwing out all of Van Eych's trophies, Miss Daniels. That includes you."

She flinched but remained tall and proud. Her icy blue eyes searched his, confirming he was serious.

As the heart attack that killed your meal ticket, he conveyed with contempt.

She turned away, and loss unexpectedly clawed at him.

He didn't have time to examine it before she pressed the door closed, remaining inside. Inexplicable satisfaction roared through him. He told himself it was because he would get the fight he craved, but what else could he expect from a woman of her nature? She didn't live the way she did by walking away from what she wanted.

Keeping her hand on the doorknob, she tossed her hair back and asked with stiff authority, "Who are you?"

Unwillingly, he admired her haughtiness. At least she made a decent adversary. He wiped the taint of dust from his fingertips before extending his hand in a dare. "Aleksy Dmitriev."

Another brief hesitation; then, with head high, she crossed to tentatively set her hand in his. It was chilly, but slender and soft. He immediately fantasized guiding her light touch down his abdomen and feeling her cool fingers wrap around his hot shaft.

He didn't usually respond to women like this, rarely let sex thrust to the forefront of his mind so blatantly, especially with a woman he regarded with such derision, but attraction clamored in him as he closed his hand over hers. It took all his will not to use his grip to drag her near enough to take complete ownership, hook his arm across her lower back and mash her narrow body into his.

Especially when she quivered at his touch. She made a coy play at pretending it disconcerted her, but she'd been sleeping with a man old enough to be her grandfather. Acting sexually excited was her stock in trade. It made him sick, yet he still responded to it. He wanted to crowd her into the wall and kindle her reaction until she was helpless to her own need and he could sate his.

Disappointment seared a blistering path through his center. He wanted her, but she'd already let his enemy have her.

Aleksy Dmitriev released her hand and insultingly wiped his own on his tailored pants, as if her touch had soiled his palm.

Clair jerked her hand into her middle, closing her fist over the sensation of calluses and heat. He was hot. In every way. All that masculine energy and muscle was a bombardment. She didn't want to react, especially to someone who wanted to *fire* her.

She dragged at her cloak of indifference, the one she'd sewn together in a school full of spoiled rich kids. "What gives you the right, Mr. Dmitriev, to take away my job?"

"Your 'job' is dead." His curled lip told her what he thought her job was.

"I'm a PA," she said tightly. "Working under the president. If you've taken ownership, I assume you're moving into that position?"

"On top of you? A predictable invitation, but I have no use for his leavings."

"Don't be crass!" she snapped. She never lost her temper. Poise was part of her defense.

He smirked, seeming to enjoy her flush of affront. It intensified her anger.

"I do real work," she insisted. "Not whatever you're suggesting."

His broken eyebrow went up. They both knew what he was suggesting.

"I manage special projects—" She cut herself off at his snort, heart plummeting, suddenly worried about her own very special project. The foundation was a few weeks from being properly launched. After last week, she knew the building she'd grown up in was badly showing its age. The home needed a reliable income more than ever. And the people…

"Clair, are you okay? You're more quiet than usual," Mrs. Downings had said last week, catching her at the top of the stairs where she'd been painting. They'd sat on the landing and Clair hadn't been able to keep it all in. Mrs. Downings had put her arm around her, and for once Clair had allowed the familiarity, deeply craving the sense that *someone* cared she was hurting.

She'd come away more fired up than ever to get the foundation off the ground. She had to keep people like Mrs. Downings, with her understanding and compassion, available to children with the same aching, empty hearts that she had.

"Are you shutting down the whole firm?" Clair asked Aleksy with subdued panic.

He turned stony. "That's confidential."

She shook her head. "You can't let everyone go. Not immediately. Not without paying buckets of severance," she guessed, but it was an educated one. There were hundreds of clients with investments managed here.

"I can dismiss you," he said with quiet assurance.

Another jolt of anger pulsed through her, unfamiliar but invigorating. "On what grounds?"

"Not turning up for work last week."

"I had the time booked months ago. I couldn't have known then that my employer would pass away right before I left." And she would have stayed if Victor's family hadn't been so cutting. If someone, anyone, had said she was needed here.

"You obviously cared more about enjoying your holiday than whether your job would be here when you returned."

The annual blitz of cleaning and repair at the home was the furthest thing from a holiday, not that he wanted to know. "I offered to stay," she asserted, not wanting to reveal how torn she'd felt. With her world crashing around her here, she'd been quite anxious to escape to the one stable influence in her life.

"The VP granted my leave," she continued, scraping her composure together by folding her arms. With her eyes narrowed in suspicion, she asked, "Would I still be employed if I'd stayed?"

"No." Not a shred of an excuse.

What a truly hateful man! His dislike of her was strangely hurtful too. She tried hard to make herself likable, knowing she wasn't naturally warm and spontaneous. Failing without being given a chance smarted.

"Mr. Turner assured me before I left that another position would be found for me. I've been here almost three years." She managed to hang on to a civil tone, searching for enough dignity to disguise her fear.

"Mr. Turner doesn't own the company. I decide who stays."

"It's wrongful dismissal. Unless you're offering a package?" She hated that she tensed in hope. She knew exactly how marketable her skill set was: barely adequate. Going back to low-end jobs, scraping by on a hand-to-mouth existence made her insides gel with dread. This job had been her first step into genuine security.

The Russian tilted his head to a patronizing angle. "We both know you've enjoyed the full package long enough, Miss Daniels. If you haven't set aside something for this eventuality, that's not my concern."

"Stop talking like I was—"

"What?" he demanded, baring his teeth. "Victor Van Eych's mistress? Stop acting like you weren't," he snarled with surprising bite. In a few long strides he was at his desk, flipping open a file, waving a single sheet of paper. "Your qualifications are limited to typing and filing, but you're occupying an executive office." Another sheet flapped in the air. "You're paid more than his personal secretary, but he still needed one because you were dedicated to 'special projects.'" He cracked out a laugh as he snatched up the next record. "You live in the company *flat*—"

"In the housekeeper's wing because it's one of my duties to water the plants," she defended, hearing how weak it sounded even though Victor had made it sound so logical.

"The janitors who dust the place can water the plants. You're a parasite, Miss Daniels. One who's being pried off the host. Take the day to pack your things."

A *parasite*. She was doing everything in her power to pay back the system! This job had been a golden egg, but she'd tried not to take advantage of Victor's generosity. Now she was finally on the brink of being able to help others instead of focusing on her own struggles—something she wanted not for the recognition, but to support children like what she'd once been—and he was calling her a parasite?

"You reprehensible, conscienceless…" Her voice dried up, which was probably best. She was shaking and liable to get personal. Mention that scar, for instance.

"Conscienceless," he repeated through lips that peeled back in a snarl. He closed her file and took up a memo of some kind. "Do you even know what you've been sleeping with? Read that, then tell me who is conscienceless and reprehensible."

CHAPTER TWO

ALEKSY TOLD HIMSELF he was only confirming that she'd actually left. He was not looking to run into her. Nevertheless, the part of him still prowling with a sense of anticlimax would leap on another chance to verbally tussle with her. Until she'd read the memo, paled, then walked out in stunned silence, Clair Daniels had been—

Forget her, he ordered himself again, but it wasn't easy. Her type was usually fair game. He didn't mess with marriageable women, just the types who enjoyed physical pleasure and material wealth over love. Clair had obviously fallen into that category, asking if he was offering a package. She'd been royally peeved when he turned her down, displaying the kind of passionate anger that suggested an equally passionate—

Stop it. He was here to take ownership of one more acquisition. That was all.

He keyed in the entry code to the firm's penthouse and stepped into generic opulence. The plants looked very well tended. Unfortunately that was the only thing recommending the place. It was the height of modern convenience. No expense was spared in the white leather furniture or silk rugs over marble tiles, but it lacked…

Traces of her.

Absently stroking his thumb along the raised line on his

chin, he strolled through a dining room that held no fresh flowers. The white duvet on the master bed was undented. The bathroom was not decorated with intriguing lingerie. In the kitchen, the pantry shelves were bare of all but the minimum staples. She'd vacated so completely, it was as if she'd never lived here at all.

How, then, would he find—

He caught the faint sound of a feminine voice through a wall and cocked his head, instantly alert. Moving past the refrigerator, he found an unlocked door to a laundry room. On the opposite side another door opened into a narrow kitchen, where the scent of toast lingered. Beyond, in a modest lounge peppered with colorful throws, unopened mail and abandoned shoes, Clair Daniels stood. She had her back to him as she finished a call. Her pert bottom and slim thighs were mouthwateringly silhouetted by clingy yoga pants.

The internal wolf that had been pacing restlessly inside him leapt to the fore, exploding his heart in his chest and slamming hot blood through his limbs. He was furious to find her here, but he smiled.

She hung up, turned and screamed.

Clair clapped a hand over her mouth as she recognized the Russian. As forbidding as he looked, as frightening as it was to have a man appear in her private space, she instantly knew she wasn't in real danger. At a very deep level, she'd been expecting him. *That* unnerved her, but she ignored it.

Dropping her hand, she accused, "You scared the life out of me!"

"It wouldn't have happened if you'd left as you were told." He no longer wore the suit jacket and tie from earlier. His fog-gray shirt strained across his chest, barely containing his big shoulders and thick biceps. He'd turned up his sleeves, revealing strong flat wrists and a ruthlessly simple gold watch.

She had an urge to touch his arm to see if it was as hard as it looked, which was ridiculous. Men fell into two categories for her: *Get lost* and *Friends is friendly enough.* She'd never been silly over boys and had always found women who went hormonal a bit irritating. She was capable of noticing a man with nice abs or a handsome smile, but she didn't get hot and weak-kneed. Ever. Especially over men who came on so strong. This quivery, oversensitized version of herself was not her.

And yet she watched with fascination as he moved with masculine grace, bending his arm and glancing at his exclusive watch, then flicking his gaze toward her bedroom door where her unpacked suitcase stood against the wall. "You've packed at least."

"I haven't *un*packed from being away." She shouldn't take such pleasure in throwing defiance at him when she was falling into desperation, but it gave her ego a boost to let him know she wasn't bowing and scraping under his every word. She didn't like what he was doing to her and wanted to make it stop. Under no circumstances did she want him to know how much power he was wielding over her.

"Well, that saves time, doesn't it?" he said with false pleasantry.

"Whose? Yours? Are you here to throw me out?" It wasn't even five o'clock. She'd started calling hotels but had wasted precious hours trying to find a workable solution for the foundation first. She had survived starting with nothing before, but she couldn't bear to let down people whose hopes she'd already raised. The trustees needed to run the home, not spend all their time scrambling for funding. She was stuck, but she didn't want him to know how desperate she was. "Why didn't you just send the clown who threw me out of my office?"

His arrogant head went back. "You can't mean Lazlo?"

"The lowbrow who said, 'I'm to assist you if you require it'? He might as well have grabbed me by the collar and thrown me into the street."

Although she had to admit it had been less humiliating to stuff her few personal items into her laptop bag and make a quick exit than try to explain while saying goodbye to everyone. She'd been shaken by what she'd read in the memo and hadn't wanted to speak to anyone while it sank in. Victor, the man she'd put so much stock and trust in, had put on far more fronts than having a young blond mistress.

"I'll remind him to be more sensitive next time," Aleksy said.

"Next time?" she repeated with a kick in her heart. "He's here?"

"No, we're alone."

Her stomach quavered. She folded her arms over her middle, trying to project confidence when she felt gullible and stupid. "Well, I'd rather deal with him. At least he doesn't sneak up on a person like a thief."

Aleksy's golden-brown eyes flashed a warning. "I bought the company fair and square and entered a flat I now own. You're the one with no right to be here."

"It's a job perk!"

"It's a love nest. One the firm will no longer support."

So this was about money. She had deduced as much. He must have bought the firm believing its worth to be higher and only learned that Victor had falsified returns after the purchase went through. He didn't have to take out his bad luck on her, though. They were both victims of Victor's ruse.

"You know, if you let me keep my job, I could pay rent

and this unused apartment could generate income, rather than be an expense," she suggested.

He narrowed his eyes, displaying thick eyelashes. "How long have you been here?"

"Over a year."

He moved through her small lounge with calculating interest, probably adding up the value of her few possessions. The place came furnished, but the faded snapshot of her parents in the cheap frame was hers. Her father's pipe stood on the mantel above the gas flame fireplace. The items were all she had and didn't come with real memories.

He jerked his chin at the pipe. "I'm surprised you let him keep you in here. A woman with your *assets* could have pressed for the main prize." He turned his head.

She ought to have been offended, but her body betrayed her. Heat flooded her under his lingering stare. Her breasts became tight and sensitive and her thighs wanted to pinch against a sweet tingling sensation high between. She was compelled to wet her parted lips with a stroke of her tongue.

His cynical lift of an eyebrow stabbed her with mortification.

"That pipe was my father's, not Victor's." She moved to snatch it up, as though that were all it would take to whisk away the pulsing attraction disconcerting her. "I never—" She cut herself off and tightened her fist around the pipe. "I signed a confidentiality statement," she finally said, lifting her chin to see him better.

He was so looming and intense with not a shred of compassion for a naive young woman who had wanted to believe she'd been noticed because she worked hard. Aleksy Dmitriev was far above her, not just in wealth and education, but in confidence and life experience. Part of her was intrigued, but their inequality raised her barriers. It killed her to beg guidance off him, but she had to.

"I'm sure you would know better than I whether such agreements are meant to be binding after a death. With your being the new owner, are you in a position to insist I disclose—"

"I insist," he commanded, flat and sharp. "Tell me everything."

"Well, I don't know anything of national import. Don't get excited. I'm just sick of you accusing me of sleeping my way to the top when I didn't. Victor was impotent."

He took her chin between his thumb and curled finger. "Don't lie," he warned.

She lifted her free hand, intending to shove his disturbing touch away.

He caught her wrist in midair, but what really held her immobile was the ferocious flare of gold in his eyes. His irises glittered with more demand than this situation warranted. It made her still out of curiosity.

"Why would I lie?"

"Because you know I don't want you if he's had you."

She sucked in a shocked breath and instinctively tried to pull away.

His grip on her wrist flexed lightly to keep her close. "That wasn't really what he was hiding, was it?"

Clair was plunged out of her depth, body reacting with alarm, mind splintered in all directions by what he'd said about wanting her.

"I—I didn't know until today that Victor was hiding anything," she stammered, trying to ignore the detonations of nervous excitement inside her. "I thought he was exactly what he looked like. A successful businessman." She tried to resist looking into his eyes, but once his stare caught hers, she couldn't look away. Her nerves seared with something like fight or flight, but it wasn't fear. The danger here was subtle. Sexual.

"How did you meet him?"

"Who are you? Interpol?" She longed to move away, disturbed beyond bearing.

"Tell me," he insisted, not releasing her.

"He needed something after hours. I was working late in the file room." She begrudged making the explanation but wanted him to believe her. Sort of. *You know I don't want you if he's had you.* It was such a Neanderthal thing to say, but it made her insides quiver. "I found it and he said I was the sort of person the top floor needed."

"I bet he did." His thumb moved into the notch below her bottom lip. He tilted her face up, into the fading light from the window. His gaze stroked her face like a feathery caress, taking in features she knew men found attractive, but she sensed evaluation, not admiration.

It shouldn't matter, but it undermined her confidence. Her looks were all she had unless she managed a miracle with the Brighter Days Foundation, and losing her job had quashed that.

"I didn't think his motive was romantic. He was old." She tested his grip on her chin, but he held fast, making her vibrate with nerves and awareness. It took everything in her to suppress her shivers and pretend she barely noticed his touch. "When I did realize he wanted people to believe we were together, I told him I wasn't interested and he said I didn't have anything to worry about. He wasn't able to make it with any woman, but he didn't want people to know. He said if I was able to keep a confidence, I'd have a good career ahead of me as his PA. I needed the money and it wasn't like he was grabbing me all the time or anything." She pointedly moved her fist with the pipe into the center of his chest and pressed. "Unlike some men."

His touch on her face changed. His fingers fanned out and he stroked his palm under her jaw to take possession of the side of her neck, thumb lightly grazing her throat.

The tender touch stilled her, not just because it was unexpected but because it felt so nice. She didn't encourage people to touch her and hadn't realized how cherished and important it could make her feel. Her lashes wanted to blink closed so she could focus completely on the lovely sensation.

"So you took him for all he'd give you and never put out for any of it."

"It wasn't like that." He made it sound ugly when she hadn't taken anything. "The raise and job title were his idea. He suggested I move into this flat because he held receptions and cocktail parties in the main suite. If people thought we were together, that was their assumption. Maybe neither of us corrected it, but all I did was work for him."

"What kind of work? Hostess duties? Attending functions as his escort?" His lip curled. "Why on earth would people get the wrong impression?"

"He was a widower, so yes, I was his date. But he also put me in charge of forming the firm's charitable foundation."

"Ha!" He released her with a lifting of his hands in rejection. "Van Eych help the less fortunate? Now I know you're lying."

"I'm not." The words rushed out, but a sense of loss washed over her as well. *Let him believe what he wants to believe,* she told herself, but if she was allowed to set the record straight, she wanted to, especially if he'd fired her because he thought she was involved with Victor. Maybe he would reconsider if he believed she hadn't been. Maybe that's what he'd meant when he'd said he didn't want her if Victor had had her.

Dismay squirmed through her. She didn't want him to

want her physically, did she? No. She was trying to rescue the foundation. If there was even a remote chance of keeping her job, and keeping the foundation alive, she had to try.

Veering from him on shaky legs, she found her laptop bag and unzipped it. "You won't have seen it on the books because it's not up and running, but I can show you…"

Most of her records were on her laptop and it took forever to wake up, but she had a slender file with proof of the logo she'd recently approved. It wasn't the fanciest letterhead, but it gave the foundation an identity and made it real. Her heart pounded with pride every time she looked at it. She showed him.

"'Brighter Days'? It looks like a child drew it." He barely glanced at it.

"It's supposed to! It's an organization that provides funding to group homes and offers grants to orphaned children so they can develop independence."

"By underwriting their lives?"

"By providing support of many kinds!" Insulted, Clair whipped the file closed. "You obviously don't know what it's like to be without parents or you'd have some empathy." As she tucked the file back into her bag, she let her hair fall forward to screen how wounded she was by his cynicism.

"Or maybe I do and I didn't have the luxury of handouts to help me find my way. Maybe I managed on my own." His tone was dangerously quiet.

The truth in the hardened brass of his gaze made her hesitate. The thought that he might have shared some of her struggles struck a chord of kinship in her, but he emanated aggression, provoking her defensive response.

"So did I," she challenged. "I'm still capable of wanting to help others."

His hard laugh cracked the air. "Van Eych gave you this

flat, a manager's salary, and countless other favors for *that* face." He pointed at her features, then let his gaze traverse insultingly down her narrow shape. "Among other attributes. Not for any smiley face you drew on the sun. Hardly pulling yourself up by your bootstraps."

He acted as if this illustration was all she had to show for her year of research and meetings and planning. Impotent fury threatened to engulf her, but to let him see he could get under her skin was handing him a weapon he didn't deserve to hold.

"I don't care if you believe me," she said stiffly. "You're obviously a bully who kicks people around for the fun of it. If you'd like to wait in *your* flat next door, I'll clear out of this one by midnight."

Such an ice queen, walking into the bedroom as though she wasn't daring him to follow. Throwing out the bait that she'd never let Van Eych have her. He wondered how she'd homed in on the one reservation he had against her and dismantled it so effectively. A depth of experience in getting what she wanted from men, he supposed. Look at the way she had singled him out as the top dog this morning, making a play with one bold look before he even knew her name.

He almost didn't care whether she had given herself to Van Eych, so long as he possessed her, which left him oddly defeated. Van Eych had stolen everything from him: not just his parents and home, but his youth and looks and his right to a normal life. No matter how Clair was connected, he ought to want to bury her, not bury himself in her.

He told himself her defiance provoked him. A man who'd conquered as many challenges as he had was internally programmed to trim the claws of a spitting cat and show her he wasn't the easy dalliance she was used to. She wouldn't be the biddable sex kitten he was used to either, but that made the thought of having her all the more exciting.

Listen to him. He knew better than to trust her, but he was halfway into bed with her anyway.

Pulling out his mobile, Aleksy texted his PA, then held his breath. He had the truth in seconds and swallowed back a howl of triumph. Her sugar daddy hadn't been capable of making physical demands. That made taking her not just acceptable but imperative.

He pushed open the half-closed door and found more evidence to support her claim. She was moving clothes into a laundry basket set atop a narrow, single bed. There was something very youthful and innocent about her. He imagined Van Eych had been feeling his age—and beginning to feel the pressure of Aleksy's running him to ground—when he'd discovered Clair in the file room.

Clair was just the old man's type: young and pretty, angelic in looks but not in disposition. Van Eych had had women on the side even during his marriage, so it came as no surprise that he'd wanted to maintain the illusion of virility into his later years. The inability to fully enjoy Clair must have churned like bent nails in the old man's gut.

If only he were alive to hate Aleksy for this. A wicked smile of enjoyment pulled Aleksy's mouth. "The medical records confirm what you say. Van Eych was limp."

She sent him a glance that tried for boredom but held an underlying flutter of nervous tension. "I told you, it doesn't matter to me what you believe."

"It matters to me." He hooked a hand over the top of the doorframe, anchoring himself so he wouldn't press forward into the room and take what he wanted before they'd outlined the terms. She had maneuvered a very profitable situation out of a criminal-class schemer. He couldn't underestimate how conniving she could be.

She grabbed a hooded jacket off the suitcase near his feet. As she folded it, she hid her expression and any chance of reading her thoughts, but he heard the wheels turn.

He took in the unpacked case as he waited for her to make the next move, distantly wondering where she'd been for a week. With a real lover perhaps, but other men didn't matter. She had never belonged to Victor. That was the important piece here. The thought of taking her for himself kindled a hungry fire in him. It was an approximation of the victory he craved, and he *would* have it.

With possessive satisfaction, he toured her shape, stoking the heat of anticipation as he hit narrow feet in bronze ballet slippers and climbed up slim but shapely legs. Hips that would fill his hands. A thick pullover sweater that hung loose, disguising whether she wore a bra. He'd bet she wore a snug undershirt of some kind, something that would trap the heat of her skin but still allow him to find and rub her taut nipples.

Her arm came across her breasts, forcing him out of his fantasy. Her blue eyes were wide, her lips parted. A blush of awareness bloomed across her cheekbones. She knew exactly what he was thinking and even though she was acting shocked, she wasn't repelled. Her lashes dropped to hide her eyes, but she flirted light fingers through hair that looked as shiny and silky as gold tassels on a scarlet cushion. Her chest rose in a shaky little pant and she ran her tongue over ripe lips.

It struck him that she wasn't accustomed to wanting the men she used.

He chuckled, delighted not only to have the upper hand, but to have her delectable body fall so easily under him. "Go ahead, Clair," he taunted. "Ask me if offering to share that bed will persuade me to let you stay in it."

CHAPTER THREE

FOR SOME REASON Abby's note from this morning came back to Clair.

I miss waking up with you.

Clair didn't allow herself to be an idealist. She knew better than to wait on Prince Charming, but her insides twisted all over again. She'd had invitations to sex before, even considered a few, but something had always held her back. Fear of letting down her guard. A sense of emotional obligation that wasn't comfortable. Never once had she heard anything so blunt and tactical.

"I thought you believed me when I said I wasn't sleeping with Victor."

"Victor, yes. No man at all?" He was three thousand percent confident, laconically filling her bedroom doorway with his primed body. "You're what? Twenty-five?"

Clair closed lips that had parted with indignant denial.

"Twenty-three," she muttered, which was still long in the tooth to be a virgin, but she was stuck in a catch-22. She had thought she ought to save herself for someone she cared about, but she shied from any type of closeness. Opening up was such a leap of faith. Handing your heart to someone put it in danger of disappointment at the least and complete shattering at the worst. The right man hadn't come along to tempt her into taking the risk.

This man shouldn't tempt her, but sex without the entanglement of feelings held a strange allure. She suspected it would be very good sex too, not just because he looked as though he knew his way around a woman's body, but because her own seemed drawn to his, sense and logic notwithstanding. He made her hot.

It was driving her crazy. She didn't know how to cope with it except to pretend the reaction wasn't there. Shaking out the T-shirt she wore to bed, she folded it against her middle and said frigidly, "What makes you think I want to sleep with you?"

"You've managed to convince me you're capable of honesty, Clair. Don't start lying now. You want me."

He could tell? How? Humiliated, she avoided her own eyes in the mirror opposite, not wanting to see the flush of awareness he obviously read like a neon sign.

"That bothers you, doesn't it?" he mocked. "That you're attracted to more than my fat wallet?"

"What wallet?" she scoffed, ducking an admission that she was reacting to anything. "All I heard was an offer for one night in exchange for what, one more day here? You said I was selling myself short earlier. Surely a man in your position could do better than that."

Her words didn't take him aback, only provoked a disparaging smile. "You want the penthouse."

"I didn't say that," she protested.

"Good, because the sale closes tomorrow."

Her insides roiled. She really was homeless. She didn't let him see her distress, only blurted, "You work fast."

"Believe it."

Her belly tightened at the resolute way he said it, and

quivered even more when she saw the gleam of ownership in his eye.

"Well," she breathed. "I can hardly ask you to share this bed if you can't arrange for me to stay in it, can I? Pity." Her false smile punctuated her sarcasm.

"I'll provide you a bed. One that's bigger and...sturdier."

A jolt of surprise zinged all the way to the soles of her feet. He wasn't supposed to take this seriously. *She* wasn't.

She clenched her hand around the edge of the laundry basket as if it were a lifeline that would lift her out of this conversation, but for some stupid reason, her gaze dropped to his open collar where a few dark hairs lay against his collarbone. She imagined he was statue perfect under that crisp fabric, with sharply defined pecs and a six-pack of abs. His hips—

Good grief, she'd never looked at a man's crotch in her life. She jerked her gaze away, mind imprinted with a hint of tented steel-gray trousers. She blushed hard and it was mortifying, especially when she heard him chuckle.

"I don't even know you," she choked, wanting it to be a pithy rejection, but it was more a desperate reminder to herself that this was wrong. She shouldn't be the least bit interested in him.

"Not to worry, *maya zalataya*. I know you."

That yanked her attention back to him and his supremely confident smirk.

"You're waiting for me to meet your price. Let's get there," he said implacably.

"That's so offensive I can't even respond."

"It's realistic. If you were looking for love, you wouldn't be living off an old man, allowing people to think you belong to him. I don't need hearts and flowers either, but I like having a woman in my bed."

"Your charm hasn't landed you one?"

He shrugged off her scorn. "I'm between lovers. The takeover has kept me busy. Now I'm tallying up my acquisitions, preparing to enjoy the spoils."

"Well, I don't happen to come with this particular acquisition." She kneed the side of the mattress. "I didn't have to share this bed to sleep in it and I had a paycheck besides. Don't throw that look at me!" she snapped, hackles rising when he curled his lip. "Victor was going to underwrite the foundation, and it—"

"By how much?" he broke in.

"Pardon?"

"How much was he going to donate toward 'brightening your day'?"

"He— You— Oh…" She ground her teeth, glaring at his impassive expression. Planting her hands on her hips, she stood tall and said clearly, "Ten." That ought to make him realize how seriously Brighter Days had been taken.

"Million?" His eyebrows shot toward his hairline.

"Thousand," she corrected, startled. She could dream of having millions at her disposal, but Victor's promised funds would have been enough to keep the doors of the home open until she raised more.

Aleksy removed his mobile from his pocket. "You do sell yourself short. We'll add a zero to that and call it a deal."

"What?" she squeaked, but he was already connecting to someone, speaking Russian, then switching to English.

"Daniels, yes. You have her details through payroll? Perfect." He ended the call.

"What did you just do?" she gasped.

"The transfer will complete in the morning." He pushed his mobile back into his pocket. "Come here, Clair."

She stayed where she was, aghast. Infuriated. Was it

wrong to be dazzled and elated, as well? Oh, what she could do at Brighter Days with a hundred thousand pounds!

"That's—" She cleared her throat, recalling he was under the impression he'd just bought her. Her stomach turned over, except...well, it wasn't with the repulsion she expected. It was like peaking on a roller-coaster track and feeling the car drop away while she hung suspended and breathless. She bottomed out quickly, though, rattled by the way the world began whirring by as the situation picked up speed. She didn't know which way was up. She wanted off.

"That's a very generous donation," she choked, blindly scrabbling up her folded T-shirt. She snapped it out and creased it into a messy rectangle against the bedspread. "I'll issue a proper receipt for the full amount after I've moved it into the trust account."

"Do whatever you want with it. It's yours. Now let's find more pleasant surroundings. I'll send someone to finish packing your things."

"The transfer hasn't cleared." Terror provided the quick retort, but it felt incredibly good to lob it at him. Better than revealing how thoroughly he mixed her up. "And given that you repulse me—"

"Do I?" He launched from his lazy slouch in the doorway. She only had time for one backward stumbling step before he'd clamped hard arms around her, pulled her into the wall of his chest, then crushed her mouth with his.

Claw his eyes out, she told herself, but aside from the fact that her arms were trapped between them, the sensation of his mouth closing on hers was too remarkable to reject. He was domineering and inexorable, but this wasn't punishment or force; it was—

Hot. Sexy. Enticing. She instinctively parted her lips under the angle of his firm ones, and his tongue speared wetly into her mouth, shooting such a jolt of pleasure through her that her knees buckled. She moaned and lifted her chin, seeking another thrust and another. Rocking her mouth against his and moaning again when his hand moved to her bottom, crushing her against the hard ridge at his hips.

It was unfamiliar and overwhelming, but she wanted to cry, it felt so good to be wrapped in strong arms, mind blinded to all but the pleasure flaring up from her abdomen, filling her with a blossoming sense of rightness. She didn't know she was moaning with gratification until he drew away and she heard her own mewl of distress.

With a final nip of his teeth over her swollen lips, he released her, letting her crumple with dazed clumsiness onto the bed's pillows.

He made an adjustment to himself, his stature powerful as a warrior's, his harsh breath moving through parted lips, the grim line softened by the sheen of their kiss. "We can wait until morning if you really want to play hard to get, but I don't think you do."

"I do," she gasped, struggling to sit up. The laundry basket tumbled off the narrow bed, dumping all her packing onto the carpet at his feet. "I don't sleep with men for money. I'll transfer the money right back to you. You can't force me into bed with you."

"I don't have to," he said on a snort, shoulders pinned back in a hard flex. "You just proved you want to." He paused to let her absorb what she couldn't deny.

An awful telltale heat suffused her, making her dig her fingernails into the edge of the mattress. It was true, she wasn't immune to him. He kept effortlessly brushing past the invisible shield that usually protected her and branding himself against her core.

"So what if I do? My instincts are warning me that it

would be a bad idea," she told him, holding his gaze and trying to listen to those instincts even as everything in her reached longingly toward him. She could barely think of anything but sating this unfamiliar hunger when he looked at her as if he wanted to flatten her onto the bed and finish what he'd started. Her breath stuttered and her nipples contracted to tight, painful points. All of her felt magnetized toward him, but she stayed put, maintaining the distance.

Something flashed in his eyes. Frustration maybe, but it had a flicker of desperation that quickly dissolved into triumph. "And of course there's your reputation. Wouldn't you like to preserve that?"

She frowned. "Sleeping with you would ruin it!" Her voice came out throaty and oddly tinged with anticipation. She was struggling for logic, but all she could wonder was, how would it feel to have him on top of her? Inside her? An earthy part of her desperately wanted to know. No one had ever made her feel so much, and the feelings weren't emotional and painful, but physical and exciting. Thrilling. Her lips were still burning, aching for the return of his.

She didn't even know him.

But she wanted to. From the second he'd stepped off the elevator, she'd been wondering who he was. Her online search had turned up dry details about his business interests, nothing about his background. Where had he come from, besides the biggest country in the world? Why had he singled her out? Why did she react to him like this?

"You read the memo," he said, interrupting her thoughts with grating flatness. "A full investigation has been launched at the firm. Anyone found to have colluded with Victor's illegal activities will be terminated. I expect more than a few rats to jump ship before they're fired."

It took a moment for his statement to penetrate. She knew she wasn't a rat, so she hadn't been frightened. Until now. "I didn't know what he was up to," she reminded him, experiencing the stabbing sense of being falsely accused. "You don't think people will say I was fired because— I would never take what I didn't earn!"

"Says the woman who just accepted a hundred thousand pounds for a charity that doesn't exist."

"I didn't ask for that!" She scrambled to her feet. "You'll never prove any wrongdoing on my part."

"Nevertheless, you've been sacked. People will draw their own conclusions. Something you're comfortable with, I believe?"

"That was different! And if I slept with you after seeming to be with Victor, I'd look like—" The biggest gold digger in the world. Her heart plummeted.

"Better to be called what you are than presumed a criminal. I'm well known for drawing a hard line against cheaters and thieves. I wouldn't have one in my bed, and the world knows it. Sleeping with me would clear your name, whereas walking away would heighten speculation. I don't think you'd find another patron after that. Not one able to keep you in the style to which you've grown accustomed."

She wouldn't find a job frying chips with rumors of lawbreaking dogging her. "*You* could clear my name! You only have to speak up."

"Make it worth my while," he countered, not bothering to hide his superior enjoyment at having her exactly where he wanted her. He really was conscienceless.

"Why are you backing me into a corner like this?"

"Why are you fighting me when you know you'll enjoy it?"

"*You* won't," she blurted, shoulders hunching. Her appalling lack of experience would bore him out of his skull before the first act was over.

Triumph flashed in his eyes and a satisfied smile drew

the corners of his mouth back, revealing a wolfish grin. “I have no problem communicating what I like, and you seem receptive. We’ll do fine together,” he assured her.

She folded her arms, fingers plucking self-consciously at the cables knit into her sleeves. The thought of his laughing at her for being a virgin didn’t appeal, but she had to tell him. “Look, I’m not…what you think I am.”

“What I think,” he said, nudging aside a pile of tumbled clothing as he stepped closer, “is that you’re something Victor wanted.” He clasped her arms above her bent elbows, gently straining them backward so her breasts arched into his muscled chest.

She gasped, stiffening in shock, hands splaying over the ridges of his ribs, fingertips unconsciously moving to trace the powerful cage beneath warm fabric. Rivulets of heat poured through her taut abdomen to a place where need pooled, making her flesh tingle and ache to be touched. “Wh-what?”

“Victor couldn’t have you and that means I must. Do you have a passport?”

She couldn’t think when he touched her, but couldn’t draw away, trapped by his strength and her own weakness. But he was talking as if she were mere spoils of war.

“Did you travel with him?” he asked with exaggerated patience.

“I was supposed to, but he died before I went anywhere. Go back to that bit about why you…” She couldn’t bring herself to say “want” when it sounded as though the sexual attraction drowning her wasn’t affecting him. She shivered in a hot-cold shudder of uneasiness while blood rushed under her skin, flushing warmth into her chest, making her breasts feel swollen and sensitized. Her hips longed to press into his, seeking the hard length that had nudged her when they kissed.

He knew what he was doing to her. A smug gleam lit his narrowed eyes as his gaze dropped to her lips. He started to lower his head.

Jerking hers back, she gasped, "I haven't agreed." But did she really want to step onto the street at midnight with her meager possessions and become one of the homeless? Her few shallow friendships were all with people she worked with. They wouldn't take her in for fear of losing their jobs. She didn't have a cushion of savings, just a credit card she couldn't pay off if she didn't have an income.

The direness of her situation began to hit home. At least this afternoon she'd been sure she could find some kind of menial work, but not now. Any character reference out of the firm after today would be career-stoppingly negative. Flicking a look from his set jaw to his penetrating eyes, she whispered, "You're a real piece of work, you know that?"

"I lost my redeeming qualities years ago," he agreed, something dark flickering in his gaze. "Which means there's no appealing to my better nature. Make this easy on both of us and give in, Clair."

She was tempted to. She didn't have anything to lose and no one to answer to while he was dangling—what? A night? A reprieve at any rate, one that advertised a fringe benefit of physical satiation she had never expected to want. The emptiness of a one-night stand was, well, empty enough to make her ache, but she wasn't in the market for a real relationship, so…

"Why extend your takeover to include me?" she asked in a voice more husky than the disparagement she was aiming for. "Didn't you get enough out of scooping up the firm from a dead man?"

"He was still alive when I started proceedings and no, I didn't get anything near what I wanted. Don't make out like you're some kind of prey just because you're used to being the predator. You get to keep the money," he taunted softly.

"No matter what?" The jerky toss of her head was supposed to convey brash confidence. The question was real, though. She couldn't help being seduced by the prospect of running the foundation her way, without needing approval on every detail. Without having to reveal that each of those details touched her personally and that was why she was fighting so hard for them. "I'm not into anything kinky," she warned. "If you're looking for someone to spank you, move along to the next girl in the secretarial pool."

"I'm not the submissive in any relationship," he assured her dryly. "I like straight sex and lots of it. I don't hurt women, ever, if that's what you're dancing around asking. I might play with dominating one, controlling her…" He flexed his hands on her elbows, making her breasts press into his chest.

Excitement returned with a spear of pleasure straight into her loins. She gasped.

"If she likes it," he murmured.

She struggled, but he held fast and to her chagrin the short tussle only caused her heated desire to kindle into a shivery anticipation. His vital strength was incredibly sexy and she must have had a kinky strand after all if she responded to having pleasure forced upon her. No guilt, she supposed.

"Too bad the money hasn't cleared," she said with breathless regret. "Go back to your own suite. I'll talk to you tomorrow." After she'd had time to talk herself out of the rash agreement she was considering.

He slowly let his hands release her, his fingertips oh so slightly brushing the sides of her breasts, making need pierce her belly and leaving her shuddering with longing.

"So you can disappear with my money? I don't think

so. Van Eych might have been teased into giving without return, but I don't tolerate cheats or thieves. Fetch your passport and we'll take whatever you've left in that case. I have properties around the world. Lady's choice where we go, but by the time we land, you'll have your money and then—" He skimmed a proprietorial glance over her. "I'll have you."

CHAPTER FOUR

"I'M LOSING MY home at midnight," her soft lips pronounced before tensing with acrimony. "I need to pack. Traveling will have to wait." There wasn't an ounce of self-preservation in her as she matter-of-factly righted the laundry basket and heaped the tumbled clothing into it.

"Don't test me, Clair. I'm not nice."

She straightened with a flushed face, all out aggression blasting at him in a way that had him planting his feet.

"What do you want me to do? Leave my things for the new owners to throw in the trash? Exactly how much do you want from me besides my job, my home and—" She clamped her lips over whatever else she almost said. Her mouth trembled briefly and for a moment there was a cast of startling defenselessness to her.

It was gone before unease could take a proper hold on him, hidden by the shift of her body away from him. Her stiff shoulders were proud. "You're the one who sold this place out from under me. Stop complaining that it's cutting into your plans."

She was acting like an amateur.

Aleksy narrowed his eyes on her back, always aware when women were trying to manipulate him and occasionally willing to allow it when it suited his end purpose: primarily to get the physical release his body required. If

Clair was attempting to wring guilt out of him, she was being predictable and hopelessly misguided. If she didn't appreciate how powerful and absent of empathy he was, he'd demonstrate.

With one call—in English so she'd understand it—he swept away her stall tactic.

"The brawny and coldly efficient Lazlo again?" she asked without turning.

"He's enlisting a young man you might know. Stuart from accounting? He's proving to be extremely cooperative. A stickler for procedure. Stuart will make an inventory of your property and put it in storage at my expense."

"Stuart from accounting wants to paw through my underpants drawer? And run back to the office with what he found in my medicine chest?"

"Not if he intends to keep his job." Aleksy didn't like the way she paled and liked even less the thought of some flunky fondling her undergarments. His hands tingled to cradle her in reassurance. He shook off the unfamiliar urge. "Gather your personal things if it will put an end to this delay," he muttered. "You have one hour."

In the end she chose Paris, but not for the reason he thought.

"The city of lovers," he'd said ironically, the timbre of his voice stirring her blood. "Of course. A perfect weekend retreat."

Weekend. The word punched low, gushing delicious heat through her abdomen.

She shook off the reaction and bit back an explanation that she'd picked Paris because she could get home on her own steam if she had to. Not that she had a home to come back to, but flying back to London from Cairo or Vancouver or Sydney would destroy her shallow savings.

As they traveled, she focused on budgeting for a new flat and where she'd start looking for a job so she wouldn't recall the way Stuart's Adam's apple had bobbled when he found Aleksy in her flat.

Aleksy had curved a possessive hand against the back of her neck and said, "I don't date my employees. Clair is no longer with the firm."

Clair had lifted a disillusioned *Could you be more blunt?* expression to him.

Aleksy had quirked his split brow in a *Want me to be?*

She'd left without saying a word, her guilty blush burning her cheeks, aware that he'd sealed her fate. Her reputation as a tart was solidified and *so* much better than criminal. That made her squirm, but she'd learned to shield herself against judgment long ago. No, it was the way he'd gotten into her head so easily that really disturbed her. It made her feel vulnerable.

"Clair."

His touch turned her from staring out the car window, once again opening that invisible gateway through her defenses. His intense personality whirled into her psyche like a restless summer wind, scattering her thoughts and inducing an instant, fluttering sensuality that reached toward everything in him.

"We're here."

The lights of Paris came to sparkling life around her. The scent of rain-damp streets smelled promisingly fresh as he left the car. The strength in his hand as he took hers to help her exit made her heart trip in a nervous rhythm against her breastbone.

She paused as he steered her toward a building, turning her face up to the sprinkling black sky to take in the facade of elegantly lit stone. It wasn't a towering structure of glass and steel, but an old-world walk-up with wrought-iron balconies and planter boxes already blooming with spring. "This is very—" *charming*, she almost said "—nice."

"It's a good investment," he dismissed.

The statement chilled her. "If you're so keen on good investments, why did I hear you dumping all of Victor's properties?" He'd been positively ruthless, speaking harshly into his mobile as she'd moved through the flat collecting her few sentimental items. He hadn't taken any losses that she could discern, but he hadn't seemed concerned with making huge profits either. "I'm sure his family would have kept what you didn't want."

"His sons kept enough," he said bluntly, pausing on the top landing to open a door by punching a code into the security pad. "I left them their homes because they have innocent wives and children, but they knew enough about how their father made his fortune that they didn't fight my takeover. I didn't have the evidence to prove Van Eych's crimes until the firm's accounting books were in my hands. Now the truth will come out and his sons will change their names to escape any connection to him."

His mouth curled into a cruel smile as he held the door for her.

Foreboding crawled through her veins. "You think it's funny to cause the severing of family ties?" Everything in her castaway upbringing was appalled.

"Funny? No. Justified? Yes."

She stepped into a room lit with intimate golden pools, but she didn't take it in, too caught up with looking for a crack of humanity in his unyielding expression. Until now she hadn't worried what would happen to her, aware only that if she walked away from Aleksy's money, she'd always cringe with regret. Orphaned children needed a voice and it wasn't as if she could find support for the foundation elsewhere. Victor was gone and who else would sponsor it if rumors started up that its founder had been in collusion with a white-collar criminal? No, if she didn't do this, the foundation was history, but reality hit as the door clicked shut behind them, loud and symbolic.

Aleksy Dmitriev was a hard man. Not cruel; she believed him when he said he didn't hurt women. He'd already demonstrated that he held himself to specific, sharply defined ethics. But he wasn't merely detached like her. She deflected emotions, but he didn't feel them at all. That made something catch in her. Apprehension, but empathy too. What had made him so devoid of a heart? Had he ever had one?

Did it matter? She belonged to him regardless.

Her heart sank, taking her last chance of protest with it, leaving her feeling naked and defenseless. *You're not naked yet,* a lethal voice whispered in her head.

"Dine out or in?" he asked, his accent raspy on her sensitized nerves.

Her breath stuttered and she struggled to catch it, not realizing she'd been holding it. Part of her would rather get the main event over with. It was late enough she was growing tired, but she was also wide-awake with nervous anticipation.

His nearness, the power of his intense glance, stole her voice. His hair had flattened into a dark helmet under the light rain. A shadow had grown in on his square jaw, accentuating everything male in him. She was ridiculously weakened by the sight. Her gaze should have been flashing a back off. Instead she studied his mouth, recalling the feel of those full lips moving with erotic control over hers. Her fingertips itched to trace the smooth curves that were uncompromisingly masculine, yet wickedly sexy.

"This stubble will burn if I kiss you the way you're begging me to," he said in a growled voice that slammed her back to reality.

"I—" She strangled on denial, mortified enough to jerk out of his hypnotizing aura and move across the room.

"I'll shower and shave. You put on one of those cocktail dresses you asked me if you should bring. I want to see your legs."

She threw him a livid glare, but he disappeared down a hall. What did she have to be angry about anyway? She'd sold herself into his control, hadn't she?

Clair gripped her elbows, hanging on to her composure with bruising tightness, taking in her surroundings to turn her mind from her precarious situation. The lounge was enormous, tiled in marble and divided into sections with area rugs and attractively arranged furniture. Everything was decidedly masculine, the writing desk set in the corner surrounded by enough space to accommodate its charismatic owner. The rest of the flat took up the entire top floor of the building, incorporating half a dozen smaller flats into a single sprawling living space that one man couldn't possibly need.

She had thought Victor obscenely wealthy. She shook her head, reminding herself that the real test of a person's class came from his character, not his possessions. Problem was, Aleksy guarded himself even more closely than she did. She wondered what kind of man lurked beneath that polished granite exterior. One who would laugh her to the curb when he realized what a novice she was?

Stop it. Steadying her knees and pulling her shoulders back, she resolved not to be intimidated. He could laugh all he wanted, but she had her own principles: loyalty, a debt of gratitude and a personal honor that demanded she live up to her word.

She was terrified, but she'd sleep with him because she'd said she would.

Her luggage was gone from his room when he emerged from his shower.

It was an unexpected slap in the face for Aleksy. Women never rejected him. Given the math Clair had scratched into a notebook on the plane, he had considered their deal more than sealed; was she now trying to get out of it?

Snatching up his mobile, wearing only a towel, he strode from the bedroom to the empty lounge. Down at the far end of the flat, as far as she could get from his master bedroom, the door was shut. He pushed through it, noted her open suitcase on the bed and heard the hair dryer click on in the bathroom.

The release of tension in him was profound—and aggravating.

Get a grip, he ordered himself as he returned to his room. She was only a woman, the same as all the others he'd taken into his bed. Yes, there was a certain satisfaction in claiming what Victor had wanted, but Aleksy had been patient enough to hunt that man down over two decades. He ought to be capable of waiting a few more hours for this final conquest.

The short flight to Paris had been unbearable, though, the drive from the airport eternal. She'd been quiet, almost as if trying to hold herself behind an invisible shell, while his senses had been homed onto her presence, for once hungry to learn about his partner, but he hadn't wanted to reveal his curiosity.

He didn't want to feel it. She shouldn't be drawing him in this strongly.

When she'd turned that look of longing on him after they arrived in the flat, it had taken everything in him to keep from leaping on her. Whether it had been a tease or real, he had ached to accept her invitation like nothing he'd ever wanted, even his lifetime of revenge. He'd controlled himself because any weakness for women had always been a distraction he couldn't afford. He wouldn't let a habit of a lifetime click off like a switch, but he'd been near panting in London when she'd thrown down her condition that the money had to clear.

His saving grace had been that she had been panting too; it was affecting him. The women he usually went for enjoyed sex, but with Clair the chemistry was notched to maximum. She might have an agenda, but her desire was interfering with it. It was an unbelievable turn-on; it enthralled him.

Surely once he'd had her the mystique would dissolve though. It had to. This obsessiveness was intolerable.

He stepped into black jeans and tugged on a light gray pullover, returning to the lounge, where he made a few calls while pacing off his restlessness, mercilessly tying off his need as he waited for staff from a nearby restaurant.

As he waited for Clair.

Clair forced one foot in front of the other and stepped into the lounge, tensed for the impact of Aleksy's inspection. He was on the phone, his face and body in quarter profile.

She had expected one of his disturbingly penetrating looks, but found herself doing the appraisal, going weak as she took in the length of his back and the way his jeans hugged the shape of his backside and outlined his muscled thighs. He stood with his long legs braced and shrugged a shoulder, drawing her attention to the powerful layers of muscles bulging beneath the wool. She imagined exploring light fingers over the textures of cashmere, swarthy neck and short, damp hair and had to strangle a moan of longing.

He finished his call and turned to strip her deep purple slip dress with hungry eyes. It was the same look he'd given her this morning, just as carnal and without the safety net of an office full of people to prevent him acting on his desires.

The assessment acted exactly as powerfully on her, pinning her feet to the floor and making her realize that for all her rationalizations about helping orphaned children, the real reason she was here was this: she wanted to be with him. It was a frightening admission after a lifetime of convincing herself she didn't want or need anyone.

"Lovely," he said, languidly climbing his appreciative gaze from her exposed knees to her carefully composed expression.

Her stomach contracted under the impact of his undisguised sexual intention.

"Victor liked it." She didn't know why she said it. Perhaps to keep him from guessing how utterly he held her in thrall, but it had a glacial effect on him.

He narrowed his eyes and said chillingly, "Be very careful about throwing his name at me, Clair."

Uneasiness wafted over her along with confusion. She had pushed that "spoils of war" unpleasantness to the back of her mind, but it came flooding forward now.

A knock on the door kept her silent.

He opened it to uniformed staff. They turned one end of the dining table into an intimate candlelit cove, setting out covered plates and pouring wine. Soft music came on and fragrant flowers complemented scents of orange sauce and rich braised duck.

Unsteady in her heels, Clair moved forward to the

chair Aleksy held for her, trying to frame her suspicion in a way that didn't demean her any further than she already was.

When they were alone, she cleared her throat. "You said earlier—" Was it only a few hours ago they'd stood in her flat setting out terms for this arrangement? What was she *doing!* "You said that you'd been targeting the firm for some time. Victor was under considerable stress leading up to his heart attack. Was that from the takeover?"

The implication behind her simple question crashed and reverberated in Aleksy's head, as swift and unexpected as the knife that had cut the line into his face. A dark maelstrom of emotion threatened, the kind he hadn't allowed himself in years. He fought it back, master of everything he felt or didn't feel, but it shocked him that she'd almost pulled something out of him that he no longer allowed. Chagrin. Loss. Rage.

"Are you accusing me of murdering him? Intentionally?" He was able to keep his tone impersonal, but she didn't mistake the threat beneath. She paled.

"N-no." Her voice was weak.

"Because I've been targeted for takeovers many times. It never raises my blood pressure. Van Eych knew what was coming and may have grown hypertensive, but that's because he didn't take care of himself. He lived as if an overweight, sedentary lifestyle would never catch up to him." His entire body ached with tension.

"I know. I told him—"

"I don't want to hear what you told him," he snapped with a slip of control that made her jump. "I know more about the man than I ever wanted to. Now I want to forget him. I want his entire existence obliterated."

He was revealing more than he intended to, but it would put an end to any more infuriating remarks regarding Victor. He glared at the elegantly simple dress that showed her delicate curves to perfection, offended that Victor had paid for it, that anything about the man had ever come in contact with her.

She sat primly, cowed by his temper into holding her hands in her lap, her spine straight, her eyes downcast. He didn't apologize; he wanted the message driven home that this topic would never be revisited again.

"Well," she said with quiet impertinence. "That certainly answers the question I was really asking, which was whether you had a grudge against Victor."

"A grudge?" Aleksy choked on the inadequacy of the word, but what did you call it when you knew a man was responsible for your father's death? For your mother's slow, painful decline? For your own self-destruction? He swept his clogged throat clean with a swallow of wine, suppressing anguished thoughts. "Yes, Clair, I had a grudge."

Aleksy's posture was casual, but his stillness spoke of extreme tension. There was nothing to be read in his expression beyond the startling prominence of his scar.

Clair realized she needed to tread softly, but she had to ask, "Why?"

"He knew. That's all that's important."

"Not to me," she protested.

The corner of his lip quirked. She realized he knew what was really bothering her. "You struck the deal you wanted. Do you hear me asking why it was important to you?"

He'd already made it pretty clear he didn't care about her motivation. This was commerce, not romance, but the worry drilling a hole in the pit of her stomach was that he didn't really want her. Obviously he was attracted to her to some degree, but she didn't want to be a *thing*. She wanted her first sexual experience to at least be sensual, not a twelve-point inspection and a stamp on the windshield. What happened when she turned out to be less than the high-performance ride he was used to?

"I just want to understand. You didn't want anything to do with me when you thought I'd been sleeping with Victor, but when you learned I hadn't, you coerced me into this arrangement. If you're on a mission to collect all of Victor's possessions, why count me among them? And why sell them off as quickly as you acquired them?"

His jaw hardened at the word *coerced*, but he only said bluntly, "To dismantle what he built. To expunge his mark on the world."

"Well, I won't let you dismantle me." She grew hot. "I wasn't his. You don't get to erase *me*."

"He thought you were his," he shot back. "You let the world think you were."

"It doesn't mean you can treat me like—"

"Property?" Bracing his elbows, he leaned forward so she had to jerk back. "Why do you care? You got what you wanted. I'll get what I want. There's no conflict."

There was, but apparently only to her.

Drawing a deep breath, she picked up her fork and said stiffly, "Just so I'm clear…You don't care whether the things you've acquired are to your taste. You only want to hold them long enough to devalue and unload them?" Looking him in the eye was an act of supreme courage, especially since it made him bare his teeth in an uncivilized grin.

"You get to keep the money, Clair. You'll walk away satisfied that your bottom line has benefited, I promise. Now let's change the subject."

"I think you just did," she muttered, staring at food she had no appetite for as she tried to sift through the mixed emotions of being physically infatuated with a man who promised to give her pleasure while only taking a cold helping of revenge for himself.

His attitude hurt her and she didn't want him to have that power. She wanted to be unaffected and remote, the way he was.

"Did I?" he responded with throwaway sarcasm.

"Yes, you did." She set down her fork with a clatter. Trying to eat was pointless when she was so consumed with nerves. She could sit here waiting out the minutes until his stupid money came through, trying to reimagine this into something more meaningful than it would ever be, or she could have sex with him and be done with it. It didn't matter if he didn't feel anything, she told herself. She had always preferred superficial connections over something deeper. Right?

Right?

"Let's do it now," she decided shakily.

Her statement arrested him. "Why the sudden change of heart?" he asked, narrowing his eyes.

Her pulse raced, but she ignored it, determined to be as *cool* and impervious as the women he was no doubt used to. "Because unlike an island villa or a vintage car, which have no say in life, I am a human being capable of making a choice. I want to complete this transaction so I can move on."

She rose and left the table, heading toward his room without looking back, unable to hear if he followed because her ears filled with a whooshing sound. Her whole body trembled. She halted when she saw the intimidating expanse of his bed.

What was she doing? A cold chill of doubt washed through her. She couldn't be so casual about stripping naked and letting a man into her body.

Fingertips grazed her spine, making her flinch. He lowered the zip of her dress before she clutched at the drooping front, panic whirling her to face him.

He scooped her to his chest, trapping her arms between them as his mouth captured hers. One hand streaked from her waist to slide beneath her elbow, where he cupped and firmly massaged her breast.

The dual sensations of fierce kiss and possessive, intimate touch hammered her with a pulse of pleasure so strong it frightened her. The situation was not just flying but exploding out of her control. She jerked her head to the side, gasping for breath, and pressed with her forearms for distance.

"You're going too fast!"

CHAPTER FIVE

HER WORDS RESULTED in a loaded silence.

She used it to gather her composure, shocked by how easily he'd stripped her of it with one soul-stealing kiss. *Compartmentalize,* she urged herself, but it was impossible when the heat of his body melted her bones and his hands flexed restlessly against her back. She had to slow him down or he'd own her completely.

Trying to hide how unnerved she was by her response, she forced herself to meet his gaze. His expression was flushed, his eyes glittering with suspicion.

"A minute ago, I wasn't moving fast enough," he growled.

Her chin automatically came forward, even though challenging him was probably the stupidest thing she could do. "A girl still wants to be seduced." It was the only thing she could think to say.

"Does she?" he asked in a tone that made her belly tremor. He held her chin and stared at her. "Or does she want to see how far she can push a man?"

"I'm not—" She tried to swallow through a dry throat. "I'm not going to back out," she whispered. "I just want a slower pace. Is that so unreasonable?" She wished she had enough experience to know exactly what kind of mistake she was making.

"Are you attempting to keep it interesting or afraid of losing control?"

His guess, so accurate, sent a startled pulse through her. Unable to control how the world treated her, she instead controlled how deeply she felt the ebbs and flows of life—but she definitely couldn't control the way she reacted to him. That terrified her.

He touched her lips. The tickling graze of his fingertip made her mouth quiver. "Tell me when you want me to kiss you, then," he taunted gruffly.

Now. She couldn't deny that she wanted his mouth. And she wanted to make a go of the foundation. If she kept that in mind, maybe she could get through this without giving up too much of herself.

"N-now." The quaver in her voice reflected her inner turmoil.

"Now?" He plucked at her bottom lip.

"Yes. But just a kiss," she cautioned, then added, "Please."

He chuckled in a way that sounded bitter and trailed his calloused fingers along her jaw, into her hair, gently threading his hand into her loose tresses as he tilted her head back.

"Since you said please..." He stepped closer and brushed a light kiss onto her neck.

She shivered as his lips moved under her jaw and up her cheek to her temple.

It was lovely, but she felt unsteady. She set her hands on his hard chest to ground herself, eyes involuntarily closing as she appreciated the patience he was showing, touching butterfly kisses all over her face, pressing the corner of her mouth and drifting away. Giving her the time to absorb each caress, the flutter of reaction it raised, and even anticipate the next.

Before she realized what she was doing, she unconsciously tried to follow him for a real kiss. His grip in her hair made turning her face impossible. The next time his heated breath flowed over her lips, she parted her own in invitation, but he left again. A whimper of dismay escaped her and she realized with a sting of uneasiness that she wasn't setting the pace at all. He was in control.

She ran restless hands over his chest. It was unfamiliar but thrilling. Hard muscle rippled with power beneath soft cashmere as she tried unsuccessfully to convey what she wanted from him.

"Aleksy." That throaty tone did not belong to her.

"Do you want my mouth on yours?" he asked in a husky growl.

She did. For all her misgivings and apprehensions, her lips were hot and sensitized, the waiting unbearable. "Yes."

He rubbed her lips lightly with his own.

A needy ache gathered hotly between her thighs. "More," she breathed.

"Show me what you want," he commanded.

A frustrated sound escaped her. She didn't know! Or did she? She wanted a proper, openmouthed, hot, swirling kiss. As crazy as it sounded, she craved the mindlessness he inflicted on her.

Lifting, she tried to show him, crushing her swollen, aching mouth against his, clinging with her lips and delicately invading with the tip of her tongue.

He stiffened.

She was doing it wrong. Failure and rejection instantly loomed, even more horrifying than the swamp of sexual excitement. She instinctively tried to pull away, but his arm tightened and she felt the answering lick of his tongue against hers. A bolt of sweet lightning flashed through her, a fierce relief followed by a warning of a storm.

She stilled, tried to pull herself together, but he boldly

took possession of her the way she yearned for, sealing their damp lips in a tight fit and thrusting his tongue against hers, spiraling her into the exciting world he seemed determined to pull her into.

Of their own volition, her hands crept up his shoulders, linking behind his neck to draw him down, encouraging him by diving her fingers into his short hair.

His arm stayed locked across her back, but he wasn't pressing her into him. She did that, not even realizing she was doing it until she felt herself plastered against him. Her dress was open, she realized, but she didn't care. Her body badly needed the pressure of his chest against breasts that seemed to swell and reach toward him, aching. A moan of longing escaped her.

"What do you want? This?" He drew one of her arms down and slid her hand beneath the soft knit, guiding her touch up his hot chest.

Startled by this new realm, she explored with rapt intrigue. His skin was like sunbaked satin, his chest hair flat and softly abrasive, his nipple small and pebble sharp against her curious fingertips. She splayed her hand, petting, fascinated, and learned quickly when he taught her the pressure he liked. She circled and flicked, feeling him jerk. Wrong again?

His arm at her back pinched her closer. "Do you want me to do that to you?" His head dipped and he caught her earlobe between his lips, sucking and sending a shocking streak of pure excitement flashing into her loins. "This too?"

She groaned at the thought of his mouth on her breast and curled her fingers against his chest, raking his nipple lightly with her fingernail. *"Yes."*

His breath hissed in. "Take off your dress, then," he ground out, loosening his hold on her and backing away.

Shaking, she dragged her hand free, grazing his abdomen on the way, feeling his stomach contract beneath her touch. He was remarkable. This state was remarkable, feeling all hot and fascinated. *Alive.*

It struck her that he would forever hold a place in her memory for this. The indelible connection was already bittersweet enough to make the backs of her eyes sting. Part of her screamed, *Run away.* The bond was temporary and would hurt to break, but she craved it all the same. Desperately. So much so that she found herself nudging the straps of her dress off her shoulders. They fell down her arms and warm silk dropped into a dark puddle over her shoes.

She was naked but for her bra, underpants and hose, all black but built for function. Her palms shyly covered the clasp between her breasts, forearms shielding the small, pale swells that peeped over the cups.

"Ask me for help with it," he said.

"I—" It wasn't that she couldn't open it. It was how real this was becoming. What if she wasn't enough for him, even for a night?

He commanded her with a look, wanting to gaze on her nude body, do things to it. The unknown scared her, but the thought of stopping was equally frightening. She couldn't move, caught in a trembling paralysis.

He stepped close and sure fingers brushed past nerveless ones. The cups released and her neck went weak. She dropped her forehead onto his chest, aware of her bra skimming lightly over her shoulders and down her back. Her breasts were exposed to cool air while her back was branded by his hot palms. She covered herself with her crossed arms, lacking the confidence to step back and reveal herself.

"Sit on the bed." He curled a steadying hand under her elbow.

She complied because she would fall down if she didn't,

but sitting put her eye level with his fly and she wasn't ready to go that far even with a glance. She looked up at him, but he was no gentleman intending to kneel at her feet. He held a look of detached intensity. A roaring sound filled her ears, the kind that warned of danger. She had inadvertently entered into a power struggle with a man who could overwhelm her without effort, but he wasn't doing it like that. He was turning her against herself. Stoking a hunger that was stronger than her natural reserve.

She clung hard to her shields but sensed he would disarm her without even trying. As easily as he caught a hand behind her knee and stroked tantalizing fingers under her calf, carrying her foot up to his stomach, tipping her onto her back.

Her heart dipped in consternation, and then she squeaked in alarm as the position parted her knees. She shot a hand between her thighs, hypersensitive to where his gaze was traveling, so tangible it was like a physical caress.

Her shoes hit the floor, *thump, thump*, barely heard over the beat of her racing heart. He reached to stroke her knuckles where she protected her most intimate flesh, his touch so personal she almost jerked her hand away in surprise.

"Let me take off these at least." He moved his hand down her thigh, stroking the translucent hose. "You want to feel my hands on you, don't you?"

"Yes, but— You're not going to undress?"

"Eventually. When you're ready." He ran his hand up to the waistband, eyes glittering with challenge while his expression was one of merciless control.

Over her or himself?

Both.

Warring thoughts crashed inside her like storm waves. Apprehension at the reality of being stripped. A moral compulsion to keep her word and go through with this. An underlying weakness of pure want. Terror at the way self-control was slipping away.

He began to draw the hose down and she lifted her hips to help him, eyes closing in denial of what she was doing, but she couldn't ignore that only her panties remained. She hid them behind her palm, knees bent to the side and locked together, breath held as she tried to imagine what would come next. And then after that.

He stood over her assessing her, proud and commanding, all the power in his court. "Do you want me to join you?"

She blew out a breath of wild laughter at his taunt. He must know how badly she wanted him and was only making her ask for it to prove a point. If she could have revealed that she wasn't ready, she would have, but it was mortifying how much she wanted to feel him on top of her. "I do." Her voice broke in surrender.

"Make room, then. When you're ready," he added, raking her body with hot, hungry eyes.

She writhed in protest, wanting mastery over herself and wanting him. Rolling onto her back, she straightened her legs, forcing her hand to fall away from her mound, the other to lift off her chest. She'd never felt so vulnerable in her life.

He set heavy hands on either side of her waist and leaned over her, taking his time studying her breasts, making her breath hitch as she felt a need to shield herself again, but resisted it. She couldn't help watching his face with a timid need for approval. She wasn't voluptuous. Would she be enough to gratify him?

His expression grew tight as he looked her over. A shudder quaked across his shoulders and it was a long time before he finally met her searching gaze.

She couldn't hide how defenseless she felt, splayed before him.

"Nice," he said in guttural English.

Nice? Her stomach plummeted at the bland word. She wasn't even sure he meant it, but was distracted from questioning him when he grasped her wrists and slid her fists above her head. At the same time, he pressed a knee between hers and opened her legs, lowering himself onto her in a blanket of soft, crushing weight.

Clair moaned in startled delight under him, twisting against his grip, but Aleksy kept her firmly clasped.

If he allowed her to touch him right now, Aleksy thought, if he didn't have a barrier between his tight hide and her downy skin, he'd lose it. It had been all he could do to find an English word to describe how exquisite she was.

He forced himself to remember that she was toying with him, trying to win a power struggle he hadn't started, but was determined to win. Stroking his free hand down her arm, past her breast, over her hip and along her thigh, he curled her calf over his lower back, resenting the wool that kept him from feeling the caress of her skin against his own. He shifted and pressed his groin tight to hers, thin layers of cotton and denim between. She was utterly at his mercy and he took full advantage, rocking himself against her, wanting her to lose control before he did.

Acute arousal hued her cheeks and glazed her eyes. Her hips lifted to increase the pressure, almost sending him over the edge, but the helpless noise she made was worth the torture she was inflicting on him by drawing this out. He was winning, but barely.

Scorching excitement seared Clair's breath from her lungs as Aleksy teased her. She couldn't move, couldn't speak, could only whimper in ecstatic sufferance. She'd kept men at a distance all her life, feeling superior to other women because she hadn't believed men really offered this kind of pleasure. She'd never felt this susceptible, but she was caving now. Completely and utterly. Breathing in his aggressive male scent like a drug.

He cupped her bare breast, his palm hot and possessive. Once a month her breasts felt swollen like this, overfull and incredibly sensitive, but never this sweet. His heavy touch assuaged the ache and incited it. Her nipple grew painfully engorged, ripening under his hot stare like a cherry in the sun. He drew circles with his thumb, massaged and shaped the swell, traced the aureole and refused to give her what she wanted. What she instinctively needed.

"Aleksy, please," she begged.

He swooped like a hawk, his masculine groan muffling as he covered the tingling tip with his hot mouth. The erotic pull almost lifted her off the bed. Moist heat flooded into her sex, completely beyond her ability to rule it. All of her became a throbbing pulse of hot need. The power of the feelings daunted her, but she reveled in them at the same time, exalted by the sense of being purely woman. When he moved to her other breast, she arched to offer herself, unable to contain her ragged moan.

His hand caressed the back of her thigh, followed the sensitive inner skin to the leg of her underpants. A sure finger slinked beneath, stroking into folds that were slick and incredibly sensitive. She had thought she knew what her body was capable of, but his touch made her jerk her hips under the intensity of pleasure. The tremendous intimacy, his confidence, the way he pressed to sustain the tantalizing peak—

"Oh, Aleksy..." she moaned.

He skimmed his touch away. "You didn't ask for that, did you?" His eyes had gone black and inscrutable. The cruel curl at the edges of his mouth told her he wasn't as innocent as he was playing. "Do you want me to touch you? Or—" He hooked his elbow behind her knee, hitching her ankle onto his shoulder. "—kiss you?"

A fresh flood of craving poured into her loins. She instinctively tried to close her legs against the betraying reaction, but she met the resistance of his muscled back.

"Yes?" he murmured, touching a kiss to her breastbone, then lower. His hot mouth opened against her trembling belly, lightly biting before he applied suction in a delicate sting of healing. "Shall I remove your panties with my teeth?"

She couldn't be completely naked under him while he was fully clothed. She couldn't. "Take off your clothes first," she gasped.

He slowly pulled away, the retreat of his body a caress that drew out the pleasure and gave her plenty of time to appreciate the cooling pain of losing him. It also brought a moment of clarity. She realized her knee lay crooked open and her panties were wet. Her stomach quivered with tension, her nipples stood taut with arousal on breasts that rose and fell with her ragged breaths.

Inhibition was gone. She didn't care how she looked or behaved, only that he continue making love to her.

Aleksy strained under his self-imposed leash. His blazing arousal burned him alive and every male instinct in him screamed to possess her. *Begged to.*

She twisted her slim body, so graceful and beguiling he had to catch back a groan of pure need. Logical thoughts disappeared from his mind. All he knew was that she tasted like summer, smelled like nectarines and ran like warm honey under his touch. Hands and mouth weren't enough to sate him. His body needed to be inside hers. His erection throbbed harder and thicker than ever in his life, desperate to spear into her.

Her taunt about going too fast was the only thing that kept him standing over her, hiding his ravenous desire behind a stoic mask while her beautiful image slithered on the spread before him. She wanted to make him crazy and it was working, but he wouldn't give her the satisfaction of knowing it. He wouldn't show her any more mercy than she was showing him. She could play games, but he would drive her to a screaming pitch, erasing anything from her mind except the same imperative eating him alive.

"Aleksy?" Her languid eyes darkened with a moment of doubt.

He let a slow grin steer across his face, liking that she wasn't assured of her lead over him. "I was waiting for your command," he mocked, peeling his pullover up and off, tossing it to the floor. There was no relief from the sweat of arousal sheening his back and chest. A conflagration of desire continued to scorch from the pit of his gut to the back of his throat, prickling his skin. Demanding action.

"Oh..." Her weak sigh might have made his lips twist in cynical amusement. It was, after all, a sound he'd heard before when he stripped, but the way she licked her lips sent a rod of need through his hard flesh, swiping other women from his mind.

"What does that mean?" he growled, barely able to find his English. "Do this slower?" He peeled open his jeans, then forced his hands to stop. One fell away to his side; the other dipped two fingers into his pocket, bringing out the condom.

Something flickered in her gaze. Confusion. Recognition. Consternation?

"You don't want me completely naked, do you?" The thought of being uncovered for the first time in his life, in *her* was enough to make him need a moment to regroup. With thumbs hooked in his waistband, he fought a complete loss of control, eyes pinned to the wink and tremor of her navel.

How he wanted her.

"Naked but protected," she eventually said, as if she thought he'd been waiting for her answer. It sounded innocent, almost as if she wasn't confident he'd get there unless she requested it. Her voice made him shudder with hunger.

He would get there. Oh, yes. Definitely.

Carefully he eased his jeans and shorts off his hips, dropping them and kicking them away, forcing his hands to hang loose, revealing none of his excruciating tension as he straightened.

She studied him in a long, taut silence, something he allowed because he was going to look at her the same way very soon. Still, he grew unbearably hard and thick under her gaze. His skin would split if she didn't let him have her soon.

"You're—" she began faintly.

He clenched the packet between his teeth and tore it open, then rolled on the latex, aware of the fine trembling that betrayed him.

"Ready," he said, finishing her sentence. "Are you?"

She didn't say anything, only looked at him with wide eyes, the reflections in them a swirl of emotions he couldn't interpret. Was she trying to tease him into insanity? He reached out to hook a finger in her panties at her hip, giving her plenty of time to slow him down.

She didn't and as he peeled them off, he had one satisfaction at least. Her nest was spun gold, darker blond than her hair, but only a little. In his periphery, he saw her hand move convulsively, but he prevented her from covering herself.

"You're too beautiful to hide, my golden one," he murmured, distantly aware he'd spoken in Russian but what did words matter when the need to touch consumed him? He drew a soft line through her curls, finding slippery silk and—

She arched as though electrified, breath hissing in.

"Yes," he agreed. "Now." He hiked her up the bed as he covered her, spreading her thighs with his own.

She reacted to the touch of his body as if he'd burned her, shrinking into the mattress before squirming to stroke herself against him, a whimper of surrender trembling from her lips. Her hands slid over him, meeting at his spine. Her legs bent to bracket his hips, and her skin was hot and soft. Delicate and feminine and enthralling.

"I didn't know anyone could make me feel like this," she whispered with an ache in her voice.

He didn't want to hear about other men. The mere suggestion shook him out of his blind, ferocious need and brought him back to reality. Was she trying to incite him with jealousy? Well, he would be the *only* man on her mind right now.

"Do you want me?" he growled.

"So much." She pushed her breasts and stomach against him, cheek rubbing his shaved one like a cat begging to be stroked.

"This?" He guided the tip of his erection to part and find the center of her.

She caught her breath and stilled.

He ground his teeth, waiting in agony.

Slowly she slid herself against him, rocking her hips, nearly exploding his mind as she teased them both with a hesitant, barely there caress. "Oh, yes," she breathed.

He thrust.

CHAPTER SIX

HER STARTLED SCREAM was quickly choked off, but it was a cry of pain.

Through his shock, Aleksy recognized that his shoulders burned under the cut of her fingernails. Engorged and rampant, his erection ached at the tight pressure stopping him from finishing his entry. Beneath him, Clair had gone stiff and taut.

For several racing heartbeats, he held motionless with incomprehension.

A strained whisper stirred the air near his ear. "I didn't think it would hurt that much."

Her words didn't fully penetrate, but Aleksy instinctively tried to pull back.

Clair squeaked and clamped her legs on him. "Please don't move."

Understanding hit him in waves. This wasn't a misjudged case of too much too soon. This was— She was—

"You're a virgin?" He was amazed he found the word. And so loudly.

She flinched. Her hands slid to his ribs, and her tangled lashes trembled with uncertainty. "Not anymore?"

"I don't *do* virgins," he bit out, but he was locked indelibly inside one. How? His normally agile brain wanted answers, but sensations crowded his ability to think. She was tight and tense, silky and hot and vulnerable. He was livid, knew this was wrong, but couldn't draw away. His body was shaking, intense sexual arousal riding his pulse, sending all the wrong signals when he was compelled to be still. This couldn't be happening. He had to stop it.

"Please don't ruin it," she said faintly.

It? He was ruining *her.*

The sharp pain was subsiding, leaving a sting and a deep awareness of the hard length lodged inside her, hot and still.

He was furious. There was no hiding from that unpleasant reality, but Clair was more caught up in how her body was trying to accommodate his intrusion. Her internal muscles flexed. An answering pulse, surprisingly erotic, made her melt around him. He settled a fraction more deeply inside her.

Her breath hitched and so did his.

She let hers go slowly, unable to look at him. His harsh *I don't do virgins* was still cutting her in two. She didn't know what to do! Her skin was still sensitized and wanting to be stroked. His penetration transfixed her. It was incredibly intimate but wickedly persuasive. She felt as if she stood in the doorway to a new understanding and desperately wanted to grasp the concept.

While she could tell he wanted to exit stage right.

Tears of frustration gathered in her eyes. "Please—"

"Stop saying that," he rasped, hands moving to cup her head. His thumbs drew circles at the corners of her eyes, rubbing the leaking dampness into her temples. "When you're ready, we'll finish this."

He sounded gruff but almost tender. The kiss he touched to her lips was gentle. Brief but followed by one a little longer. A little more thorough.

She sighed in relief. He wasn't giving up on her. As he took her mouth, she curled her arms around him, pulling him into her, wanting to feel all of him. When she tilted her pelvis, he slid home. There was a final sting, but—*oh*—such a sense of rightness. Too many sensations to pick apart and name. She was all feeling and he was part of it. All of it. She squirmed against him, filling her hands with him, seeking maximum contact while reveling in the fresh magic of being possessed by him.

He kissed her with ravenous generosity, exciting kisses that transmitted joyous signals through her, making her move against him.

Thick Russian words filled her ear as he slid his wet mouth down her neck, tucked his hand under her bottom, carefully withdrew and thrust.

It felt so perfect, so *good*. Clair threw back her head, a lusty groan tearing raggedly from her lips. She couldn't speak, could only embrace this primitive state and encourage him with ancient signals, stretching and arching beneath him, moaning her pleasure.

Urgency built, quickening their rhythm. The sensations were so acute she wanted to scream. She needed more. "Please, Aleksy, please."

With a growl, he thrust faster, offering what she craved, taking and giving, straining over her, driving her to a peak, holding her there, pushing her off…

She fell, but into flight. Breathless, soaring flight. Distantly aware of his guttural yell, she rose to skim the sun, where she burst into brilliant, ecstatic flames. It was the most delicious death until, like the sparks from a spent firecracker, she drifted in pieces back to earth.

Aleksy reeled as he left her. Dealing with the condom was his excuse, not that he voiced it, but he had to get away from her. He was spent, body twitching with exertion and coated in sweat, but he wanted her again. She was like Christmas dinner, when it didn't matter that he'd already gorged himself. Greed for more consumed him.

He splashed cold water on his face, then glared in self-disgust at his reflection, his scar standing brilliant white against his flushed skin.

Incredible, mind-shattering sex that shouldn't have happened at any pace. *You're going too fast.* No wonder she'd been so shy about surrendering to passion. And when she had…

Please don't ruin it. What was he supposed to have done? Left her frustrated and disappointed by her first experience with a man? Would that have salvaged something of the civilized gentleman in him?

As if there'd ever been anything civilized in him, he thought with bitter self-recrimination, old blades of guilt and abhorrence flashing between himself and his image. He was well aware of the primitive forces in him. He held them in check with his rigid standards, always. Shame and contempt filled him for dallying with a virgin. He'd stolen from a man he didn't even know.

How dare she put him in this position?

He moved back to the bedroom to confront his mistake and found her sitting up, the sheet knotted in her fist against her collarbone leaving her pale shoulders bare.

She looked like a bride on her honeymoon, thoroughly tumbled, lips puffy and ripe, hair tousled, expression still retaining some vulnerable innocence while her new knowledge made her skim a hesitant, admiring look over his frame.

That look was a baited hook that caught in his gut. Lower even. The erection that hadn't completely subsided pulsed with renewed life.

He hated the response he couldn't control; he refused to be led by it, especially where she no doubt thought she could take him. Planting his feet hard on the floor, he crossed his arms and stood at his full height.

"I won't marry you." His cold warning grounded out the sexual electricity still crackling in the air.

Her shoulders flinched before she steadied them. "Did I ask you to?"

"It's reasonable to assume you're trolling for a proposal with this little gesture, especially ahead of the money transfer, but forget it. I'm not the marrying kind." She wouldn't have tried this if she knew what a monster he really was.

"What little gesture?" She lifted haughty eyebrows.

"A woman's virginity belongs to her husband." He'd never forgive himself for this. Fooling around with experienced women was one thing. They had the same unclouded views he did. Innocents had expectations he would never live up to. "I didn't ask for your virginity, so don't think you can guilt me into making restitution for it."

She reddened with insult. Or anger. He didn't let himself dwell on what she might be feeling so long as he was driving his point home.

"A woman's virginity belongs to her husband?" she repeated through her teeth. "Welcome to the twenty-first century where a woman's body belongs to *her*. It doesn't look like you're saving *your*self for marriage."

"It's a good thing one of us knew what he was doing." Although he hadn't. She'd neglected to inform him of one very salient detail. She was craftier than he'd given her credit for, coldcocking him with that one.

"We all have to start somewhere. What good is waiting for a husband who hasn't once shown up when I needed him? I'm stuck with taking care of myself, aren't I?"

"And this is how you chose to do it? By throwing away your virginity for hard cash?" Precisely the type of woman he usually dealt with and yes, he supposed they had all started somewhere. He was still left with a pall of disappointment in both of them.

Astonished hurt parted her lips.

Out of habit, he mercilessly sealed over the fissure her crushed expression threatened to make in his conscience, closing himself off to any emotional appeals. Best if she understood he had no heart, but then something in him stirred. Perhaps she really was romantic enough to believe this sort of thing led to a lifetime commitment. The weight of being unable to live up to that expectation settled heavily on his shoulders.

She surprised him by masking her hurt. As though shrugging into a coat, she pulled on an air of dignity. "I made a choice that was mine alone to make. I'm not the marrying kind either."

He snorted. Innocents like her dreamed of a family. If his own family were alive, they'd expect better of him than the way he was behaving right now. Of course, if they were alive, he'd still be an innocent like her.

"You don't know me," she said with quiet assertion. "You don't even want to. I'm only spoils of war to you. I trust your grudge is satisfied and you'll leave me now?"

The cool, pithy words struck his abdominals like punches. That wasn't what this was. Despite hating himself for not realizing sooner that he was her first, the basest male part of him was already anticipating tasting her shoulders and neck again, stroking the warm silk of her back and thighs, making her writhe against him until she was ready to take him into her. And it had nothing to do with revenge.

He didn't want to leave her—which stunned him—but

she had to be tender. He hadn't been as gentle as he would have been if he'd known… if he'd *known*...

His skull threatened to split under the pressure of conflicting imperatives. He had to leave her. For now.

CHAPTER SEVEN

CLAIR WOKE IN an unfamiliar place, mind blanking with alarm before her memory rushed back. She sat up, still in Aleksy's bed, still naked and very much no longer a virgin. Anxiety quickly faded to relief as she saw she was alone. She couldn't have dealt with him *and* her mental disarray. Stunned disbelief bounced off crazy elation and crashed into an inferno of embarrassment.

Hugging her knees, she tucked a hot face into them and tried to countenance how she'd let Aleksy do all that to her. She hadn't grown up with a lot of affection; nor did she possess any long-denied, deep-seated needs for physical closeness.

Yet she'd reveled in Aleksy's caresses, giving herself over to him without inhibition.

Her heart wrenched as she recalled that the singular experience had cost her his respect. What kind of throwback had such archaic views on virginity? His judgment and contempt had hurt, not that she should care what he thought, but a weak part of her did. She wanted to know he'd enjoyed their coming together as much as she had.

Physical satisfaction was secondary for him, she knew. He'd taken her to strike at Victor and he'd walked out right after, his interest in her gone with the same lightning speed he'd developed it. No one had ever wanted her for the long haul. It was silly to imagine that a man like him, who could have anybody, would be any different.

The door creaked, startling her.

He caught her unprepared for the impact he had on her. He was still wearing the crushed pullover and snug jeans from last night, but he wore confidence like a visible aura so radiant she needed sunglasses. His hair was damp, the short cut combed uncompromisingly to the side. She knew how those soft strands smelled. How they felt between her fingers. Against her breasts.

His gaze locked with hers as though he read the memories she tried to repress. She died a little at being incapable of locking him out, nipples hardening with remembrance of his mouth, loins pooling with excitement for him.

It was distressing to react this strongly, to relive these sensations without him even touching her. It was a massive invasion of privacy. Against her will, her mind zeroed in on that safe moment when they'd been unequivocally linked. He'd been a lover then. She'd felt cherished, not bare and self-conscious like now. Everything in her yearned toward that memory like a flower seeking the warmth of the sun.

But that man was gone. This was the man with the grudge. To him she was a pawn on a chessboard to be tipped over and taken with ice-cold deliberation. And he'd done it.

This was the get up and get out moment, she supposed, her pulse racing.

"Hungry?" He sounded ironic, his deep voice abrading her taut nerves.

Was he taunting her for skipping dinner in favor of sating herself with him? It was cruel. She dug into her deepest reserves of composure, the way she'd done when the school bullies had taunted her.

"I could eat." She lifted her chin and kept her gaze steady, ignoring that she was on fire inside. Other women were capable of relegating sex to something as mundane as chatting over coffee. She needed to be exactly that unaffected. She needed to get this awkward morning after finished and get out of here. "Why? Do you not know how to boil your own egg? You need me to do it?"

His eyebrows elevated a fraction at her pert challenge. His golden eyes looked deeply set into hollows darkened by a sleepless night. She was so startled by the thought that this powerful man might have lost sleep over her, she let it go as if it were hot.

The impression dissipated as he said with casual arrogance, "I pay the housekeeper to cook—or in this case deliver pastries."

"Oh. I would have liked to walk to the patisserie."

A flicker of surprise crossed his expression, followed by a purse of his mouth that made her bite her lip. He didn't want to stroll hand in hand down the Champs-Elysées and she hadn't meant to sound as if she was longing for romance either.

"I've never been to Paris. I'd like to visit a patisserie for fresh croissants at least once in my life," she defended, embarrassment stinging her cheeks. "But that's fine. I'll be out in a moment." She shifted her feet to the edge of the bed, signaling she needed privacy to rise and dress.

He didn't move.

Because there were no secrets from him behind this sheet. Perhaps he had sent his housekeeper out and come to wake her for a different reason. Her heart tripped and her fragile poise slipped. She swallowed, mind casting with indecision. She knew she shouldn't want to sleep with him again, but she did. Weak longing stole over her even as she searched his expression for his intention.

He gave nothing away as the silence grew loaded. Finally he entered the room, coming around the bed. She tensed, but he passed her by, stepping into the bathroom long enough to reach for something off the back of the door. When he returned, he draped a pewter-colored robe over the foot of the bed. "Take your time."

He left and she let her breath out in a whoosh, staring at the closed door, wondering why she felt so forlorn. In the space of twenty-four hours the man had completely taken over her world, which was intolerable. She didn't need to be completed. She was already whole. Aleksy might have tapped through her inner walls last night, but she had an infinite capacity for shoring herself up against the world. He'd simply caught her in a moment of weakness. Showered and dressed, she'd be completely unaffected.

She had to be.

Aleksy was not used to sexual denial. If he wanted a woman, he found one. When he had one, he *had* one. Waiting for Clair in the lounge, knowing she was running a soapy cloth over her nectarine-scented skin, was excruciating.

The proximity of her lissome body had burned in him all night as he paced the dark lounge. Taking her should have iced his vindictive cake, allowing him to discard her and move on, but he couldn't stop thinking about how exquisite she'd been. He'd thought he only wanted to mark his victory over his enemy, but she wasn't Van Eych's. She belonged to him, only him.

It was one more twist that caught him unexpectedly. He'd planned to be in London indefinitely as he drew the noose ever tighter around Van Eych's neck, putting him in a cell while stripping him of his stolen riches, but going to London had turned into nothing more than a formality because Victor had died. Aleksy's appetite for steering the takeover was gone. He could leave it to his team and go back to Russia where his own interests had been neglected far too long.

Given Clair's inexperience, he should sever their association. The deepest part of him knew that, but the rest of him rejected the idea. What would be the point in acting gallant now? Her virginity was gone. She'd given it up as a survival tactic in the face of losing her job and home. If she was going to sell herself, it might as well be to him.

It was a rationalization he grasped with surprising desperation, which disturbed him. For two decades his entire life had revolved around one thing: retribution. Taking Clair was supposed to be a facet of that, but instead she'd been an escape from it.

The stark realization unsettled him, agitating him further when he realized he wanted that escape again and again. He told himself it was timing and circumstance, that he would have found extra significance in any woman he'd bedded right now, but he didn't want *any* woman. He wanted Clair.

So he would keep her as long as it took to satiate this inexplicable want, he decided.

His resolve took a hit, however, when she appeared in a filmy white sundress a few minutes later. Her disturbing sense of purity made his heart lurch. It was not unlike the modesty she'd shown in not being able to reveal herself by leaving the bed this morning. She withheld her thoughts behind a mask, but her blond hair was a golden veil and her minimal makeup revealed her natural beauty, fresh-faced and ingenuous.

If this was going to work, she had to fit the mold.

"I'll book you into a salon today," he pronounced with the swift call to action that had made his meteoric success possible. It would also fill her day so her nearness wouldn't tempt him beyond bearing. Women always expected a new wardrobe anyway.

Clair touched her hair, her composed expression denting with confusion. "I had a trim a few weeks ago."

Aleksy resisted the urge to roll his eyes. "A fashion salon," he clarified, then added with irony, "So you can wear what I like." He held a chair at the table for her.

"Why? Taking possession of Victor's trophy wasn't enough? You need to stamp your own engraved plate on it?" A betraying unsteadiness undermined her cool challenge.

He didn't let her remark ignite his temper. "I intend to remove any traces of him from you, yes."

"For whose benefit?"

She seemed genuinely baffled, which was yet another reminder of her unfamiliarity with the way these arrangements worked.

His housekeeper brought their meals at that moment and he watched Clair withdraw even further behind her frustrating shields as she was offered tea and asked if she'd found everything she'd needed.

After Yvette left, Clair muttered, "As if this isn't harrowing enough." Her hand tremored as she helped herself to a croissant, the only betrayal of tension behind an otherwise cool demeanor.

"Harrowing." Aleksy repeated the unfamiliar word so he'd remember to look it up.

"I'm sure mornings after one-night stands are old hat to you, but this is my first. I'm not exactly comfortable with a stranger witnessing it."

He tensed. Was that what she thought? "I don't do one-night stands," he informed her quietly.

"Or virgins, if I recall. Must have been a two-for-one special."

"But you're not a virgin anymore, are you?"

She stilled. Smoldering memories darkened the blue of her eyes, igniting a lovely blush under her skin. She swallowed and looked away.

He didn't like that she would try to withhold any part of herself from him, especially that intriguing response. Forget experience. She had to know that once wasn't enough for either of them. He reached out and drew her chin around to face him.

The look in her eyes was shockingly defenseless, full of anxiety and fear coupled with deep longing. Things that stirred a deep, protective desire to comfort her with tenderness…

She jerked back, blinking away the peek into her soul, turning serious. "I need to return to London."

Her words jolted him with a startlingly strong kick of possessiveness. "Why?"

Clair's heart jammed under his intense regard. She wanted to be as dispassionate as he was, but it was impossible. Her normal ability to hold people at a distance wasn't bearing up against Aleksy's penetrating looks. She didn't even know why she was having a problem with this. She had known she was a conquest, nothing more, but she still felt vulnerable, out of her element and unaccountably lonely. Everything in her wanted to escape before it got worse.

"To find a job and a place to live," she reminded him.

It was amazing how his eyes could harden into inscrutable bronze disks that still managed to pierce like lasers. A muted hum sounded and he glanced at the mobile next to his plate. "Perfect." Turning it, he showed her the message. "Your time is mine now. Along with everything else," he added with silky danger, his gaze sliding over her like loose, velvet bonds.

Clair read the confirmation of deposit, fifty thousand into her account. Her emotions seesawed as all of yesterday's repugnance at the arrangement flooded back.

"We agreed on one hundred," she said, then inwardly shrank from her mercenary retort. But it was for the foundation, she reminded herself. She wasn't putting herself through this emotional wringer for one pound less than what they'd agreed. With a defiant lift of her chin, she used a show of mutiny to mask her shame.

"You don't get where I am without performance guarantees. What if you'd changed your mind?" Aleksy was a study of couched power, ready as a tiger to leap.

"But I didn't. I held up my side of the bargain. I expect you to do the same." She felt like one of those balls on a tilting table, rolling out of control, destined to fall through a black hole any second.

"You'll receive the rest when our affair is over."

She gripped the table. "But— I thought—" Once had been enough for him, hadn't it? Last night he'd certainly left her with that impression. "It is over, isn't it?" The hesitant question came out involuntarily. She held her breath, not sure what answer she wanted to hear. Her ears pounded with anticipation as she watched something stark and fervent flash in his eyes.

"Nyet."

No? Or *not yet*? She was so lost in trying to read his expression, so off balance by the uneven trip of her pulse that she couldn't make sense of what he'd said. And she had prepared herself to walk away today, blasé and sophisticated and only slightly scathed. Her incredulous laugh scraped her throat.

"How much longer do you expect it to last?"

He shrugged laconically. "Until I'm bored."

No. Unpredictability made her anxious. "You can't expect me to put my life on hold indefinitely."

"Consider it a lesson against agreeing to open-ended contracts."

"But—" A panicky lump lodged in her chest. All she could think was how easily he had peeled away her layers of reserve last night. She didn't know if she could withstand further baring of her inner self.

"What's the problem? You said yourself you have no rent to pay or employer to report to. Do you want me to say I'll ensure that those details are looked after before we dissolve our association? Very well. I can agree to that."

"That's not—" She searched the hard angles of his face, cringing from the vague distaste curling his lip, wondering how his twisted brain worked that he could only see her as avaricious and self-serving, not scared out of her wits because she was drifting so far over her head. "What did Victor do to you that you're like this?" she breathed.

The billowing silence told her she'd stepped over a line. "My history with Van Eych is not up for discussion. It has nothing to do with us. You and I have a strong sexual connection that needs to run its course. When it has, I'll release you and the rest of the funds."

His words sent a zing of surprise all the way to the soles of her feet. A strong sexual connection? "I thought I was paying for the sins of a man I barely knew," she charged, hands knotting under the table.

His cheeks hollowed. *"Nyet."* He looked away, fiercely controlled emotion tightening his mouth. "There is no way for anyone to compensate for that. His sins were too great."

He gave off vibes of such deep devastation, such intense pain, an unfamiliar desire to reach out caught at her. He'd only brush her away, she reasoned, startled that the impulse touched her at all. She wasn't the affectionate sort.

And yet she found herself turning over that *strong sexual connection* remark. Was she more than a tool of reprisal after all? Fluttery sensations like a million moths flooding toward a sliver of light filled her.

"Are you saying you want…*me*?" It took all her courage to step into the bottomless chasm of asking him.

He grew guarded and his eyes cut to her with a flinty look. "I want your body."

The inner door that had cracked open slammed shut. "Of course." She removed her napkin from her lap, no longer hungry. But what did she have to be offended about? She wanted him for *his* body, didn't she? Her long-term avoidance of relationships had been an avoidance of the unbearable sea of emotions that came with them. Wanting to be wanted was agonizing. She'd learned early not to let those longings take root. Skimming her gaze over his unabashedly masculine form, she recognized that he was offering her a gift: all the joys of physical engagement without a toll on her heart.

He cocked his head, amusement tilting his mouth. "How is it that a woman as naturally sensual as you are has never taken a lover before?"

Her pulse raced at how easily he'd read her yearning in one brief, unguarded glance. If she continued seeing him, she'd have to learn to keep her thoughts to herself.

"No one ever tempted me." She tried to keep her voice level so he wouldn't guess how unnerved she was at the way his powerful sex appeal kept smashing through her self-protective reserve. "And normal relationships don't interest me," she added.

"Normal?" His eyebrows climbed.

"Dating to find love. Searching for a soul mate." Profound disappointment seemed the inevitable follow-up to those quests. "You were right when you accused me of being more pragmatic than that. I don't want to live in a cave, but most people my age live the other extreme: partying and hooking up. Being Victor's platonic mistress seemed like the happy medium." She sipped her coffee, but it had gone cold and bitter, much like how she felt about her arrangement with Victor, especially now that she'd glimpsed how much pain he'd caused Aleksy. It was yet another harsh reminder that relationships—even ones with seemingly impervious boundaries—could reach inside to wound.

She should take that as a warning sign, but last night had been extraordinary. All her reasons for agreeing to sleep with Aleksy were still there along with memories that made tongues of flame lick down into her pelvis.

"Now you see the advantages in being a real mistress," he murmured in that deadly accent. He reached for her free hand, lightly combing his fingertips between her fingers before tracing a path across her palm. Her entire body jolted and a moist layer rose under his teasing caress.

She tugged her hand into her lap and tried to erase the tingling sensation by rubbing it on her thigh. She couldn't hide that he had a profound effect on her.

As if he read her response as acceptance, he nodded with satisfaction and rose. "I'll call for the car. You'll need a full wardrobe before we leave for Moscow."

"Moscow?" Her composure dropped along with the coffee cup she still held, the clatter in the saucer jarring. "I can't get into Russia without a visa."

"I have your passport. Lazlo will arrange it," he dismissed with a shrug.

"What happened to ladies' choice? I run my own life, Aleksy." She rose to grip the back of her chair.

"I've been occupied with this takeover at the expense of my interests at home," he said stiffly. "I need to return and I want you with me. Is that asking too much?"

I want you with me. Don't, Clair. Don't let that mean something.

"You're not asking," she pointed out, determined to assert herself.

"No, I'm paying for it."

Ouch. Piqued, she threw back, "Yes, you are, because I'm not footing the bill on whatever you expect me to wear."

His scarred face twisted with a smile of patronizing satisfaction that made her want to bite back her words. "I wouldn't expect anything less."

CHAPTER EIGHT

SHE SHOULD HAVE known a man like Aleksy could only come from a city like Moscow. It dominated the way he did. Its weighty buildings with their tall, imposing towers and sharp-eyed windows spoke matter-of-factly of strength and the ability to endure. The facades, scarred by history, told a story she would never fully hear.

Yet there was an unexpected idealism she hadn't expected in the archways and balconies and loving attention to detail. Even Aleksy revealed a streak of sentiment in the way he'd refurbished his living quarters with an eye to art and a respect for the past. The block he lived in had been built for high-ranking Soviet leaders, he told her when they arrived, which accounted for the amazing location on the Moskva River and enormous top-floor mansion, but the original wiring and wooden interiors had made the building a fire hazard. He'd had the entire structure torn apart internally over two years and was rebuilding to original floor plans with upgraded specifications.

That surprised her. He seemed unaccountably merciless in everything he did, utterly focused on his own interests. After their night flight from Paris, he'd spent most of today in his office down the hall, phone buzzing constantly, conversing in half a dozen languages. Yet if he'd only wanted to turn a coin with this building, he could have made simpler choices, punching out cookie-cutter flats for foreign investors. Instead, from the brief glimpse she'd caught through the replicated elevator cage, he was blending modern conveniences with charming vintage elements, offering stylish homes to his countrymen.

Most startling of all was the photograph above the fireplace in the lounge. The bride wore a modest dress, the groom a simple suit and tie. The corner of the small snapshot was burned, the colors faded, but it was set off by a wide mat and an elegant frame, so it took up significant space, speaking of its importance to the flat's owner.

She guessed from his resemblance to the groom that they were his parents. Aleksy confirmed it with a simple *da*, not encouraging more questions, but she'd found herself oddly encouraged by this evidence of a softer side in him.

Such a complex man, just like his city.

And now he'd brought her into it. *Indefinitely.*

She still felt apprehensive about letting him pressure her into going along with his demands. His strong-arm tactics didn't bother her so much as the way she'd folded to them did. She knew how to stand up for herself when it mattered. This mattered. She wasn't a ward of the state anymore and wasn't about to let him erode what autonomy she'd managed to build for herself. It was too hard won.

Nevertheless, she was here. As his mistress.

Until he grew bored and paid her out.

Flinching from that brutal inevitability, she moved away from the window and took up the two gowns again, hands shaking. She was trying to decide which was better suited for seeing the ballet at the Bolshoi Theatre—as if she had the first clue what the well-dressed mistresses in Moscow were wearing.

How infantile it had been to try striking him in his wallet

when it was so well padded. She couldn't imagine what he'd spent on her. Victor had given her a small clothing allowance and she'd bought conservative outfits that helped her blend in with those around her. She liked being unobtrusive.

Aleksy was having none of that. These gowns were daring and sophisticated, the colors bold, the designs requiring confidence to wear them well. She wasn't sure she could pull off a dress like this any more than she could cope with being Aleksy's woman.

Stop it, she ordered herself, refusing to backslide into wanting to belong to someone. He didn't want her soul and she wouldn't give it up. This was a reciprocal exchange of pleasure, unencumbered by demands for true intimacy.

"What are you doing in here?" Aleksy's stern voice made her jump.

"You startled me." Despite her previous affirmations, her knees weakened at the sight of him. Her reaction was a complex tumble of nervous excitement and an inexplicable desire to earn his admiration.

She clamped down hard on those self-destructive emotions but couldn't wholly suppress her physical response. He was still in the casual pants and button shirt he'd worn all day in his office, and his expression was downright forbidding, but her heart raced with appreciation of his fiercely handsome looks. When would he touch her again? The question had been burning in her blood all day.

"You said to be ready for eight," she reminded him, using the gowns as a shield for the lightweight silk robe she wore, glancing down at the drapes of color to keep him seeing her involuntary and immediate desire.

"I meant why are you in this room?" He moved forward and took in the open closet, the myriad empty boxes and zippered dress bags. "I instructed the housekeeper to put everything away in my room tomorrow."

Her heart dropped like a boulder from a rock face. Share his room? After living alone she was finding the idea of sharing a flat—even one as big as this—to be a hard adjustment. She couldn't breathe with him four steps in the door. No, if she was going to get through this in one piece, she needed her own space to retreat to.

"The boxes were in here, so I assumed this was my room and unpacked them." She conquered old twinges of wanting to apologize for occupying any space at all. This wasn't a foster home. He'd brought her here. She'd stay, but on her terms. "I'd like to use it," she said firmly.

He assessed the volume of clothes. "As a dressing room? Very well, but I'm not about to creep up and down the hall looking for you. You'll sleep in my bed."

Conquering a suffocating panic, she asserted, "I don't want to."

"Why not?" He turned the full power of his intense personality on her.

She swallowed, not intimidated by his power and height, but instantly vulnerable to the effects his alpha male nature had on her. At some point they'd have sex again and the recently awakened woman in her craved that so deeply she was a little frightened by the power of it, but sleeping together would have its own way of increasing her reliance on him. That wouldn't do.

"I—" The word was cut off as he drew her into a strong, careful embrace. She automatically tensed and pressed the heels of her hands to his chest, fingers still curled around the padded hooks of the hangers.

He looked down at the way she held him off, not forcing her body into his, but she sensed the firm planes of his stomach and the long, hard muscles of his thighs teasing like a warm breath beyond the fall of her kimono.

He tugged the towel from her head, releasing her damp

hair, and tipped her head back so her gaze tangled with his. He stroked her cheek, then let his caress trail into the sensitive hollow beneath her ear and under her jaw.

"I'm looking forward to tonight. I don't know how I've managed to work when all I could think about was touching you again. Feeling you under me."

Her arms pressed harder as she tried to keep his seductive words from affecting her, but everything else in her melted. This was the sensual heat low in her abdomen she'd looked forward to. She consciously closed herself off to reading any significance in his admission that she'd been on his mind, though. As he lowered his head, a helpless moan escaped her. Her hands released the weight in them and slid up to curl around his neck and into his hair. The first touch of his lips shot a jolt through her. They melded together as the kiss deepened without any insistence from him. She welcomed him with a passionate response, transported to the exciting world he'd initiated her into while trying to hang on to herself, not give him everything—

He lifted his head. They were both breathless. His cheekbones were flushed, but his eyes glittered with aggravation. "What's wrong?"

"Nothing," she murmured, aware of an internal tension that grew as he delved into her gaze. Keeping herself disconnected from the way he made her feel was hard. She looked at the sobering line of his scar to cool her blood, wondering about it.

His expression grew stony as he slid his hands over the silk gown, his palms hot through the slinky fabric, molding her back and fondling her bottom, making her tremble.

She let her head fall forward onto his chest to hide how the sweetness in his caress made her eyes moisten. She felt his hardness against her belly, urgent and thick, and caught her breath in wonder. He wanted her. *Her.*

A burst of relief made her dizzy, unnerving her, filling her with the tautness of wanting him while remaining wary of limitless intimacy. She gathered herself behind an invisible wall, before she followed through on her desire to look up and press her lips to his neck.

Before she could make the move to take this where her body wanted to go, he set her away from him and bent, coming up with the red and the blue gowns. He rejected the red with a toss toward the bed, his expression inscrutable. Holding the blue in front of her, he said with detachment, "This one. Give me thirty minutes. I'll meet you in the lounge."

Her mouth still tingled from the pressure of his. Her whole body felt light enough to fly while bitter disappointment weighed like a rock in her throat, keeping her from calling after him. She refused to beg for affection.

As he dressed, Aleksy was still trying to understand what had transpired in the other room. The fact that he was being so introspective about Clair's behavior was as irritating as her trying to hold him off.

After resisting temptation all day, he'd been unable to help going to her. Finding her in the spare room, trying to keep space between them, was an oddly disturbing rejection. Everyone gave him a wide berth, but Clair's doing it stung unexpectedly. Did she fear him? The thought galled him.

He'd been compelled to close the gap and pull her into his arms with as much gentleness as he was capable of. She had reacted beautifully, her arousal instant and obvious.

When he'd kissed her, her mouth had parted beneath his. The silk of her robe had revealed the tension in her belly and the sharp points of her nipples. Her supple body had even leaned into him. *She*, however, had not been involved.

Why not? She'd called herself practical when they were in Paris, her interest in her financial future blatant enough to assure him they were on well-defined ground. Had she read something about him that had turned her off?

The way she had stared at his scar had seemed to suggest so. Then she'd folded into him, almost as if she was ready to surrender regardless of what she thought of him, but he'd been stinging with disgrace. In one glance, she'd reminded him that it didn't matter how mercenary she was, he still didn't deserve to touch her.

Even she seemed to know it.

From inside the limo, his world gave an impression of chilly silence. The few people on the street wore overcoats and furred hats as they hurried down the street, breath fogging in the frosty air. Yet their very presence in the cold evening spoke of perseverance and a steadfast grasp on life, entrancing Clair into forgetting she didn't want to fall in love with anything, even his country.

How could she stay immune, though, when he'd put her in the center of a fairy tale? The limo stopped and Aleksy left the car, holding a hand to help her stand, so courtly he stole her breath.

He wore a tuxedo with a white bow tie and gloves. It ought to have seemed affected, but his features were carved with masculine perfection, his brow stern enough to make everything about him serious and deliberate. Backlit by an enormous, columned building with a rosy-cream glow, he was devastatingly handsome.

She stood on unsteady legs, taking in the milling crowd streaming around the frozen fountain toward the spectacular entrance of the theater. This was the world he inhabited. Miles above any she'd ever thought to visit. Her treacherous emotions lifted with excitement, caught in a spell of beauty and wonder.

As if that wasn't magical enough, his presence cut a swath through the crowd of people. One glance over their shoulder and people moved aside. Aleksy kept her pressed close to him as they climbed the stairs, coldly ignoring murmurs of "Dmitriev" and Russian phrases she didn't understand, coupled with glances at his scar.

Taking her cue from him, Clair refused to acknowledge the morbidly curious looks, pretending to be absorbed in the grandeur of the theater. She was genuinely awed. The ornamental detailing and painted ceilings looked as if they'd been finished yesterday. For a moment time slipped away and she was a nineteenth-century aristocrat carrying a fan and wearing lace to her throat. The man at her side was an arranged-marriage husband—not a far cry from today's situation at all, she thought with a wry, inward wince. He was supporting her and there was no hope for love.

An attendant approached to take her cape and Clair revealed the modern, off-one-shoulder sparkling blue dress that clung to emphasize her narrow curves and create more height than she really had. Aleksy procured them flutes of champagne and, after a brief consultation with the attendant, told her, "We have the czar's box."

She tried not to drop her drink.

As if this were any casual date, he guided her through a set of double doors that led through an ornate sitting room. Another set of doors ended on a grand balcony fit for, well, royalty.

Red velvet and gold struck her from the row of luxuriant chairs with their gilded edgings to the scalloped curtains framing the box to the auditorium beyond. A wall of balconies stretched away on either side in floor-to-ceiling rows, each separated by low walls decorated with gold leaf and glittering chandeliers. An enormous cake of sparkling crystals cast glamorous winks of light from high above, sparkling off jeweled necks and sequined gowns.

Clair sank weakly into the chair Aleksy pressed her toward. "I didn't think Russia had a czar anymore," she stammered, half fearing they'd be executed for trespassing.

His smile warmed her as if she'd gulped her entire glass of alcohol. "It's actually the president's box now. We could have used mine, but as this one's empty tonight and I'm such a valued patron…" He shrugged self-deprecatingly.

"You must love the ballet. I mean—" The way his eyebrows climbed made her rethink presuming anything about him. "You have your own box and support the company. Everyone seems to know who you are."

"*Litso so shramom*." His expression altered as he repeated the phrase she'd heard as they entered. The carefully composed lines of his face revealed nothing—which was a revelation in itself. "Scarface."

The bluntness of the moniker made her blink in shock, but she hid it, guessing anger on his behalf wouldn't be welcome.

"I'm hardly anonymous anywhere I go," he said, his jaw tensing. "And no, I don't have a particular love of ballet. Coming here is merely—forgive the ancient metaphor—the quickest way to telegraph my return to the city. Do you like the ballet?"

"I've never been," she answered, lowering her gaze as she absorbed his offhand question. Her preferences had obviously been the last thing on his mind. This was the most exciting outing of her life, yet he'd brought her here for reasons that had nothing to do with her. She had to stop wishing for more! She went back to the nickname.

Irrepressible curiosity made her ask, "Does it bother you that people see the scar, not you?"

"There's no separating one from the other, is there?" His look hit her like a face full of icy slush, his tone chilling her blood.

"I don't know," she replied, ignoring the bite of his hostility, fighting not to take it personally even though she sensed a hint of accusation in his demeanor. "Have you looked into plastic surgery?"

"Why? Does it disgust you?" His fingertip unerringly found the line of raised tissue. He drilled her with his eyes, but she didn't have to lie.

"No. I don't notice it more than any of your other features, like the shape of your nose or color of your eyes." She stopped speaking as she heard how revealing that sounded. She was stunned to realize how thoroughly she had already memorized his face: the hint of a raised bump on his nose, the wicked slant in his eyebrows, the cleft in his chin. She had to force herself not to let him entrance her now.

"It's an advantage," he said flatly. "While people are trying to decide how many of the rumors they should believe, I've summed them up and leapt three steps ahead."

"You like that it makes them nervous. Then they don't try to get close to you," she guessed, earning another baleful glance that made her breath stick. She was certain she was right, though, so much so that parts of her softened toward him as she recognized their similarity. She feared isolation, so she forced herself to find contentment in being alone. What did he fear that kept him holding people off so ferociously? Caring?

The thought was a double-edged sword of understanding and hopelessness so acute it made her head swim.

"This scar reminds me who I am and where I've been,

which is a place you don't want to go, Clair," he said in a gentle warning that made her heart batter her ribs. So he had suffered a very deep wound. Nevertheless, she *would* listen to his story if he wanted to tell her. Had he ever told anyone, she wondered?

The lights faded before she could ask. Faces below rotated to watch the curtain rise. Music swelled as *Petrushka* began to unfold with its tragic puppet, considered cruel but instead capable of emotion, trapped in a cell, unable to reach the ballerina he loved.

Aleksy loathed small talk. It was a step into familiarity that he never encouraged. Clair had been spot-on when she suggested he was happier holding people at a distance.

Scowling, he wondered what had possessed him to talk about his scar. It was a topic he usually shut down outright, but he'd been compelled to learn if it was behind the reserve she'd shown earlier. Clair was exceptionally beautiful tonight, and fresh bitterness had overcome him that he was such an unsightly match for her.

Intellectually they were on an even playing field, which was an anomaly for him. Rather than babbling inanities or barbs, she had a quiet sincerity when she spoke and displayed surprising insight. He avoided women who made him feel. He'd never had one who made him think.

Disturbed by a rush of both anticipation and caution, he forced himself to stop letting her get under his skin and instead focus on their surroundings.

He noted with twisted pride how her smile of pleasure attracted curious, admiring looks during intermission. He detested networking at any level and would have stayed in the private lounge attached to the czar's box if he could, but he succumbed to convention at these things.

With hooded fascination, he watched her greet those

who approached with seemingly sincere warmth, admiring dresses and jewelry if no other conversation presented itself. He was used to his dates sulking, or smiling as if it pained them to make the effort, leaving the weight of social chitchat up to him. Clair put people at ease and he found his own tension ebbing because people weren't so nervous—which, contrary to what she'd said, always made him impatient. Aleksy glanced at the next hovering couple, smiling as he recognized the man behind the gray beard and the woman's twinkling blue eyes. He introduced Clair to Grigori and Ivana Muratov, smoothly forcing those trying to hold his attention to move along.

After brief inquiries about their daughters and grandchildren—he had known their entire family for many years—he and Grigori became caught up in discussing politics.

"That was the chimes," Ivana warned a few moments later, touching her husband to interrupt their conversation. "Intermission is over, but this charming young lady has just told me about the charity foundation she has started. We would like to help her with that, wouldn't we? Aleksy has made a donation."

The unexpectedness of Clair's subterfuge against these of all people made Aleksy's cheeks sting with a rush anger. Thankfully the couple didn't notice, both smiling at Clair's bewildered face.

"Of course we'll match it," Grigori agreed, clapping Aleksy's shoulder with enough enthusiasm to nearly knock him off his unsteady feet. "Send me the details." With cheerful goodbyes, they hurried down the hall toward their own box.

"They seem very nice. How do you know them?" Clair lifted the most guileless eyes to him but sobered as she read his forbidding expression. "What's wrong?"

"Grigori gave me my first real job after my father was

killed," Aleksy answered. He had to school his fury with everything in him as he took her arm and led her back to the lounge. Before she could pass through to the balcony, he cut her off, closing the doors so they were alone in the sitting room.

The music rose in the auditorium and Clair lifted a nervous hand to indicate it. "The show is back on."

Aleksy turned on her. Whatever she read in his grim expression scared her, but she held her ground with more mettle than anyone he'd ever made a point of revealing his fury to.

"Why are you angry?" she asked with rigid dignity.

"Did Van Eych teach you to work a situation like that or is it a personal gift?"

She straightened as tall as she could possibly be, a pale reed so beautifully set off by the deep blue of the gown he nearly had to close his eyes against the temptation to touch her. He focused on the finery of the dress instead, on the fact that the small fortune he'd dropped on her new wardrobe wasn't enough. She was trying to steal from his friend, as well.

"What do you mean?" she asked.

"I won't let you take advantage of Grigori's generous nature." The man had been his salvation, offering Aleksy not just work, but a fresh chance. Grigori had helped a desperate young man put a roof over his mother's head while giving him the opportunity to move up the ladder toward the life he lived now. The life itself didn't mean anything, but Grigori's hand up when no one else had offered meant the world.

"I didn't expect Ivana to offer a donation." Clair managed to sound not just innocent, but hurt. "We were only chatting. She asked how we'd met, so I told her about the charity."

"Which doesn't exist!"

Clair's jaw dropped open. Rather than cower under his blistering gaze, she drew a deep, hissing breath of outrage. "Don't tell me your precious Lazlo failed to advise you of the email I sent him today? I attached the tax receipt. What?" she dared challenge as he narrowed his eyes. "You thought I asked for the Wi-Fi code so I could update my social media status to 'mistress'?"

He ignored her biting sarcasm. "I can check," he warned. "With one call."

"Do it," she choked, acting so offended as she swung away that he experienced a flash of misgiving. He shook it off and scowled at her as he withdrew his phone.

Seconds later a muted buzz vibrated in his palm. Clair's back stiffened as though the sound were the whir of a whip and she was bracing herself for the lash.

The edges of the device dug into his hard grip as he read and reread the message.

"You told him you'd print me a copy if I asked, so he assumed I was aware," he paraphrased, needing to hear it to fully comprehend it.

"You didn't ask," she pointed out, barely able to look at him.

"So it's real, this charity of yours." She even had a registered number.

That swung her around to face him. "Of course it's real! I'm not a liar. You don't truck with those, remember?"

He found himself in the completely unfamiliar state of being at a loss as he let it sink in. "I don't understand," he muttered, voice graveled by his impatience at being faced with something that didn't add up. "You gave me your virginity for *charity?* Why would you do that?"

"People like me deserve—" She cut off her outburst and struggled visibly, jaw flexing as though chewing back words she hadn't meant to voice. Flicking her hair back from her shoulders, she changed tack. "Look. I didn't want all my work to die on the vine. Brighter Days fills a very real need."

"For who?" he asked suspiciously. "Finish what you were going to say. People like you deserve what?"

Clair's jaw ached. She didn't want to tell him. Why? Because she was ashamed? Still? If she wanted to get anywhere with the foundation, she had to conquer this sense of being second class once and for all.

"Support," she answered with a swell of defiance. "When there's nowhere else to turn." She wasn't as confident inside as she acted. It had always been hard to believe she really deserved any such thing when no one else seemed to agree, but she deeply believed children like her deserved a caring home and opportunities to make a secure life for themselves. If she didn't act as their voice, they wouldn't have one, just as she hadn't.

"What kind of people are we talking about?" Aleksy asked. "Orphans?"

"Yes." It was incredibly hard to look him in the eye. Her stomach trembled as she braced herself for how the label would change his view of her.

Aleksy had vaguely absorbed that she didn't have family, but the information had only penetrated distantly. Now he sensed how deeply she felt her lack and was thrown off by her vulnerability. A pang struck him dead center of his chest so hard he wanted to rub it away.

"How old were you when—?"

"Four." She hid her flinch with a shrug, steeling her spine. This was costing her, he could see it, but she said without inflection, "Car crash. I had a broken leg and a dislocated shoulder. They died instantly."

"Why does that make you so defensive?" He had an

urge to take her in his arms, but that wasn't who he was. He didn't coddle, but he still found himself trying to reassure her. "Being an orphan isn't a crime. I'm one."

"You lost both your parents? Not just your father?" Her somber blue eyes softened with empathy, threatening to pull things out of him he didn't want to release. "What happened? How old were you?"

He was instantly sorry he'd mentioned it. "Fourteen when I lost my father. My mother lived until I was twenty. I suppose I wasn't technically orphaned." He glanced away, deliberately not addressing how his father had died. "I'm only saying there's no shame in not having parents who are still alive. It's hardly something you can help."

The irony of his assurance twisted inside him. He suffered deep shame over his father's death and the fact that he'd never been able to provide properly for his mother. He lived daily with the anguished guilt that even if his mother had survived to live as he did now, it wouldn't have cured the broken heart that had been the real cause of her withering away.

Suppressing the agonizing memories, he focused on Clair's circumstance instead, observing, "Four years old is still young enough to be adopted."

Tendons rose in taut lines against her throat as she said with stunned hurt, "That wasn't really in my control, was it?"

He might as well have kicked a puppy. He wished he could take it back, but the damage was done. She was pulling herself inward, composing herself into the untouchable woman he had seen several times now. Her skin was incredibly thin, he realized. He'd bruised her without even knowing he could do so. The way she mentally distanced herself caused an unexpected gap of agitation to open beneath his feet.

He moved forward, taking her arms in a light grip, as if he could prevent her retreat into herself.

She stiffened and her hands came up to his chest. He read the same conflicting signals of resistance and subtle, sensual melting that he'd felt in her earlier in his apartment. She liked his touch but was trying to shield herself at the same time, something he understood all too well, but she didn't have to fear him on this.

"You're right, of course," he murmured, experimenting with a light massage up and down her arms. "I shouldn't have said that. Where did you live, then? An orphanage?"

"Yes." He felt a quiver go through her, one she suppressed as she said with quiet dignity, "The home was the only real one I had. It was stable and I needed that after being in foster situations for the first few years. That's why I'm trying to ensure that it has enough funding to stay open, but I don't need the donation from Grigori. The amount you've promised is so much more than Victor offered that I can keep them going and actually support expansion. Tell Grigori whatever you like. I won't bring it up again. I'll just tell people we met in London and leave it at that." She turned her face away, lips tight.

He had dismissed her charity as a ruse when she first mentioned it, imagining that at best it was the illusion of a bleeding-heart idealist incapable of solving real problems, but the full impact of it being genuine continued to jar through him. She wasn't a gold digger; she was a mother bear fighting to protect children.

The knowledge sliced a fresh cut of ignominy through him, but he ignored it, too caught up in trying to understand her.

"You might have given me some indication," he admonished. "Why let me believe your motivations were shallow?"

"What do you care what motivates me? This isn't the sort of relationship where we talk about our scars, visible or otherwise, is it?" she challenged, pupils contracted with wounded pride.

A knot of complex emotions pulled his gut tight.

"No," he agreed. His hands unconsciously tightened on her arms.

"Good. Because I don't want you in my h-head," she said shakily, but he heard the underlying hurt.

The constant rejection in her life had made her understandably wary of intimacy, Aleksy guessed, but he couldn't stand that chilly shell she was trying to recover. She wasn't just in his head; she was under his skin so deep he could barely breathe without feeling her. Physical intimacy was the salvation for both of them, he told himself.

"How about your body?" he murmured, pulling her hips into a delicate crash against the erection that had rarely subsided since he'd met her. Sex seemed the only way to get past her shields, and he would use it, now, before she'd locked her barriers into place. "Do you want me inside *you?*"

She started with surprise and drew a sharp breath, face flooding with a sexual blush. "I— Well, y-yes. I mean, that's what we've agreed, isn't it? Um." Her words caught and faded into a husky tone of arousal. "Un—um, uncomplicated and…" She licked her lips nervously and the play of her tongue was almost a visceral stroke up his spine.

Simple. Practical. Physical.

He tried to hang on to the words as he backed her toward the divan, the need in him, once acknowledged and released, so intense his muscles began to shake. Every cell in his body ached for the pleasure she promised, but there was a primordial aspect to it that he refused to examine too closely. He wanted more from her than sexual accommodation. He wanted her to give herself to him because she wanted to, not for any orphaned children. He wanted her as ensnared by this wild passion as he was.

He levered her slight body onto the cushions and lowered himself to cover her.

Clair released a helpless whimper as Aleksy's hot mouth touched the racing pulse in her throat. Her overwhelmed senses took in the painted ceiling and the music beyond the doors. Had he locked any of them? The back of the divan offered a bit of protection if someone walked in but not much.

"Aleksy," she choked, voice thick with the conflict of wanting him so instantly she was almost willing to risk discovery and holding back because she was upset. All her internal guards were shattered and in bad need of repair. She should wait until she had a better hold of herself, but he was strangely reassuring in the way he caged her beneath him without crushing her. The way he trailed his lips across her bare shoulder, pausing to drink in the scent of her skin.

"I want everything you'll give me." The statement spurred a light-headed rush, one that nearly lifted her off the divan as he slid his finger under the diagonal edge of her bodice to reveal her breast.

His mouth found the tip and her mind exploded. His urgent demand was as exciting as his mastery, causing a thrilling flood of heat into her extremities. She wove her fingers into his hair, making him lift his head. She was desperate to own his mouth but too shy to say it.

Her body spoke for her, knee bending to bracket him into the space between her legs. He responded by stroking her ankle, her calf, her thigh. With their eyes locked in ever-intensifying connection, he climbed his hand beneath the skirt of her gown until he touched her so intimately she had to close her eyes.

That only made her excruciatingly aware of the deliberate way he tantalized her. She lodged the back of her hand against her open mouth, muffling the cry of pleasure that escaped as he caressed and teased, making her long for more—

"Oh!" He pressed into her wet core and she clenched, surprising herself with an unexpected orgasm that squeezed her eyes shut and rocked her entire body. Jagged moans refused to be suffocated.

"I'm sorry! I'm so embarrassed," she said into the paneled back of the divan, almost sobbing as he lifted her to strip her undies away.

"Don't be," he commanded, his voice thick and fierce. He rose over her, his penetration happening at the same time he took her mouth in a kiss that captured her deep groan of relief.

It was better than the first time. All sweetness as he filled her and paused, giving her a moment to accommodate his thick, hot girth. She grasped at him, certain there could be nothing better than this first deep thrust to alleviate the acute need.

Then he moved and the pleasure storm swept through her.

CHAPTER NINE

ALEKSY SHIFTED, ROLLING onto his back, snapping Clair out of her deep sleep.

Her naked back reacted to the loss of his heat like the cool, raw flesh under a bandage. She fought a foreign desire to turn and burrow into his warm strength.

Smoothing her hair from her eyes, she let her gaze find shapes in the barely discernible pattern of the wallpaper, trying to make sense of what was happening to her. She'd been so angry, so hurt at being misjudged, and positively crushed at his remark about being adoptable. Did he think she hadn't spent her entire childhood waiting for new parents? For someone to want her?

He didn't care about her struggles or pain—he'd more or less admitted it when she challenged him. He only wanted sex from her. That's all this affair was, and it should have turned her off, should have kept her from making love in public at the very least, but his touch had erased all the hurts. She'd forgotten there was such a thing as loneliness.

And the sense of connection had inexplicably remained, even when he'd wryly apologized for being unprepared with a condom and dried her belly with his handkerchief. It should have been a horribly awkward moment, but she'd found herself giggling as if they shared a secret. His tender kiss had tasted like a promise as he solicitously straightened her disarranged clothing and shielded her from the eyes of the wait staff while they slipped out of the theater, flushed and pinned together.

The drive had been a blur. She'd stared out the window without seeing anything, mind reeling, belly still quaking, skin sensitized with longing. There'd been no misgivings, just a glow of joy like an ember inside her.

She hadn't recognized the feeling as a state of sustained desire, but when he'd drawn her to him before their shoes and coats were off, she'd met his kiss with an enthusiasm that had made him groan. He'd scooped her into the cradle of his arms and carried her to this bed. She hadn't given one thought to how long she'd stay here, only that she needed to be naked with him, all of her hurts and worries forgotten.

She very much feared she was losing herself, and that was bad.

Nevertheless, when his big body jerked behind her, her pulse leapt as if they were connected by invisible, electric wires. They'd spent a long time getting to know each other's body. She'd even let him slide down her to arouse her so selflessly she'd almost died, but oh, the deliciousness of that near-death experience. When he'd risen to thrust into her, they'd locked themselves into a writhing knot of ecstasy. She'd been so exhausted and replete after their final, shuddering culmination that she'd fallen asleep without making a conscious decision to stay in his bed.

She should leave now that she'd woken, but she was reluctant, especially when he crooked his leg against hers and renewed desire tingled through her. Would he wake and love her again? Who knew she could be this insatiable?

He muttered something in Russian.

Drawn by curiosity, she rolled to face him and tried to read his features in the dark. His eyebrows were pulled together in a grim line, his jaw clenched. His long body was one taut muscle weighing down the mattress. More utterances pushed through grinding teeth.

A nightmare? Reaching out with instinctive compassion, she lightly touched the tensed muscles of his neck, thumb accidentally lining up with the ridge of his scar on his chin. “Aleksy.”

He clamped a swift hand around her wrist, the strength of his grip painful enough to make her cry his name again in a warning.

With a jolt he woke, but his grip stayed locked tight. “Clair.” He sounded…fraught, his tone demanding she answer.

“Yes, it’s me.” She tried to rotate her arm and ease his unbreakable hold. “Where were you?”

He drew a shaken breath, letting his fingers loosen, then just as quickly caught her arm again, closing around her fine bones, exploring lightly for damage. “Did I bruise you? I’ll get ice.” He released her and started to leave the bed.

“No, I’m fine.” She dropped a staying palm on his chest, startled to find it soaked with perspiration. “You’re sweating. Do you have nightmares often?”

“Never,” he replied shortly, dragging the corner of the sheet over himself, dislodging her touch as he dried himself.

Smarting from his brush-off, she curled her fist into the blankets and drew them up over her chest. “Maybe it was my being here. I was just leaving, so…” She trailed off.

He didn’t say anything.

She waited too long. Nausea clenched in her stomach as she realized he wasn’t going to protest and ask her to stay. Aghast at herself for making the mistake of fishing for signs she was needed—or at least not unwanted—she forced her stiff limbs to ease toward the edge of the bed. Funny how she had spent years conquering feelings of bereft abandonment, learning never to set herself up for it, yet the tsunami of worthlessness could sweep over her as fresh and coldly devastating as ever.

This was exactly why she avoided intimacy. He was too far inside her if he could bring her to the brink of anguished rejection this easily. This wasn't supposed to happen.

Years of practice allowed her to swallow the lump of unshed tears trying to lodge itself against the back of her throat. She wouldn't cry, refused to. She found her way down the hall to the spare room and crawled into the icy bed with dry eyes, telling herself the ache clawing at her insides was for Aleksy.

What would haunt him so badly he'd have nightmares? She'd been distracted by his misjudgment of her and the foundation earlier, but he'd said Grigori had given him his first job after his father was killed. He had shut down and diverted her by asking about her own history, but she had a feeling the touchy subject of his scar was related. The way he'd just called her name as if he'd been frightened for her stayed with her, filling her with an urge to go back and ask him about it. Offer comfort.

Rolling onto her back, she flung an arm over her eyes and reminded herself not to give or ask too much. This relationship was temporary and if she got any more emotionally involved with Aleksy, she'd be too deeply attached when it ended. Look how she was reacting to being separated by just a wall. She didn't want her heart broken when half a world stood between them.

Better to stay exactly where she would spend the rest of her life: alone.

Aleksy stared unseeingly at the frozen river, still deeply perturbed by his nightmare. He hadn't had one since his mother was alive, yet the dream and the memory it contained had ambushed him with deadly accuracy.

Except this time, when he'd heard his name, Clair's voice had called it and torment had nearly ripped open his chest.

Soft footsteps padded on the tiles behind him. Not the bustle of his housekeeper and he felt Clair's presence like a tangible force anyway. Her sexuality radiated into him, synchronizing to his own. He wanted to touch her with the immediacy that swept through him every time he was near her.

He hesitated to turn, though, dreading what he might see. He had meant to be gone by now, but his driver was caught in one of Moscow's world-famous traffic jams, so he was loitering in his own foyer, mind jammed with unwanted introspection. When he pivoted, he caught her hovering indecisively, showered and dressed, hair glittering like sunlight in icicles. She took in his suit and tie beneath his open overcoat, then the briefcase on the floor. Her eyes were underlined with bruised half circles. No sleep either? Or something else?

Apprehension made his voice unintentionally severe. "Good morning."

"Good morning," she answered. Her cloak of composure slid firmly into place, hiding anything she might have betrayed.

He felt his mouth twist in dismay, but really, it was for the best. He'd saturated himself in her last night, allowing his own well-built defenses to waver so he could draw her in as tightly as possible, but apparently letting down his guard had allowed his subconscious to come out of hiding. That was so disturbing he didn't know what else to do but run.

"You're going out?" she asked without emotion, making it impossible to tell if she was relieved or disappointed.

Her remoteness renewed the fear that had been creeping through him since the early hours. Had he said something revealing in his sleep? Was that why she'd left him for the bed down the hall?

"I'm needed at the office." He scowled at the briefcase he'd filled like a criminal fleeing the country, as if putting off facing her would change anything. There was no changing what she thought of him, only the disclosure of what that might be. "I didn't mean to disturb you last night." He watched her closely, trying to discern what was going on.

"It's fine." Her lightness sounded forced. "I needed to go to my own bed anyway."

He bit back a reflexive *Why?* Her insistence on sleeping apart from him annoyed him and he didn't understand the reaction. He usually gave his women separate apartments and left *them* in the middle of the night, but even that first night when he'd been in a state of utter turmoil, there was something satisfying in knowing Clair was in his bed. He'd looked in on her more than once, baffled by the spell she'd cast over him, but pleased with her presence.

He was a possessive man with possessive urges, he supposed, trying to rationalize how out of sorts he was. But this exaggerated reaction made him more determined than ever to ensure that this arrangement stayed on clearly defined footings. She had a place in his life and it was a narrow one.

"Invitations will be pouring in after last night. I'll call to let you know where we're going and what time to be ready." He collected his briefcase, willing his driver to ring. "I have accounts at all the boutiques on Tverskaya. Ivan will come back after he drops me and you can shop or Lazlo can arrange a private guide if you'd like to tour the city."

Clair tried not to gape, but she was still trying to process her reaction to last night's expulsion from his bed and all she could think was, *So this is what a mistress does with her downtime.*

Logically she understood that a strong man like Aleksy would hate that he'd revealed any sort of vulnerability, so she tried not to let his plan to abandon her cut too deeply. She'd spent hours last night coaching herself not to take any of what happened between them to heart. This wasn't personal; it was convenience. Sex. Good sex.

She licked her lips, trying not to get off track, but memories still crept through, warming her with insidious desire. She suppressed them, considering the shopping and sightseeing offers. Getting out sounded good, but she didn't need anything after the spree in Paris. She just wanted to clear her head and remember how to be herself.

"Don't bother anyone. I'd rather see where my feet take me," she decided.

His macho eyebrows came together like clashing titans. "You want to walk? Alone?"

The incredible sexism in the remark got her back up. "Do you think I'll get lost? I'll print a map before I leave."

"It's not safe," he impressed on her with another stern frown.

Clair dismissed that with a wave. "I've lived alone in London for five years."

"Moscow isn't London, Clair. Kidnappings are on the rise—"

"Who's going to kidnap me?" She splayed a hand on her chest, forcing a laugh, but the need to state the obvious gave a surprising pluck against her heartstrings. "I don't have any family to threaten. Remember?"

"Do you think the paparazzi at the Bolshoi haven't printed photos of the woman with me last night? Even without that you're young, pretty, well dressed. You don't speak the language. Opportunists are out there and you should never, ever underestimate what people will do for money. I don't." His scar stood out stark white against his flush of emotion.

Foreboding slithered through her. She knew then that his scar was not the result of a tragically placed ice patch and a broken windshield. Aleksy had been indelibly marked by violence. Internal brakes wanted to screech the whole world to a stop so she could somehow process that, but how? There was no erasing what had happened to him.

A poignant ache flooded her at the same time. Before she realized what she was doing, she reached out with all the familiarity that had developed between them last night. Cupping his jaw, she lifted herself on tiptoes, aware of him stiffening as she leaned into him. Her lips almost brushed the puckered line before he abruptly set her away, jerking his head back.

"What are you doing?"

His rebuff tore her in two. She winced, regretting the lapse in her reserve, but he had no idea how few people ever showed concern for her—and after whatever he'd been through…

"Thank you for trying to look out for me." She forced the words out.

He tugged the lapels of his overcoat as if he were fitting armor back into place and closed a few buttons. Glancing at his watch, he took a step toward the door, speaking over his shoulder dismissively, "You'll stay in, then? Or call Lazlo for an escort?"

Her silence made him pause. He turned another weighty frown in her direction.

Clair curled her toes in her slippers. It would be so easy to let her self-reliance crumble and allow this protective, strong-willed, incredibly attractive man to run her life.

What about when they were through, though? She'd be back to taking care of herself. She *had* to hold on to her independence.

"I'm not *your* kidnap victim." She tried to sound wry, but for some reason her lips trembled and her heart skipped a beat. "I'll go out if I want to."

"Despite the risk," he snapped, temper sharpening his voice.

"It's not that great a risk!" She folded her arms, stopping short of saying he was overreacting. Obviously his experience had taught him differently. Determined to hold her own, she reasoned, "When you want to do something, who do you ask? No one, right? Same here."

His jaw tightened. He was used to everyone answering to him, that much was clear. The precisely machined, titanium wheels in his head seemed to whir at top speed as he sought a suitable rejoinder.

"I'm not trying to be obstinate," she said, checking her flawless manicure.

"But you won't give me your word."

"It would be a lie."

With a hiss of impatience, he set down the briefcase, its weight hitting the tiles with a hard *thunk*. His mobile sounded and he answered with a staccato burst of Russian before tossing the device on the hall table and shedding his overcoat, his stare holding hers with antagonistic force.

Clair swallowed and fell back a step. "What?"

"You won't stay at home as I've asked, so now I have to take action, don't I?" He began loosening the knot at his throat.

"What does that mean? You're going to tie me up?" Genuine alarm made her retreat several feet in the face of his deliberate advance.

"It means I have to change and go with you." He yanked

his tie free and draped it over her shoulder as he passed, voice pithy and displeased, but he still made her grin as he said, "Save the tying up for after dark."

Clair reminded herself she was not behaving like a spoiled socialite. She was a fully grown adult making her own decisions, and Aleksy could do the same. She wasn't keeping him from his work. His pacing and brooding would not make her feel guilty.

She refused to set herself up for criticism either, so she took the precaution of checking the weather even though the sky was intensely blue and the sun glanced brilliantly off Moscow's blanket of snow. The modiste in Paris had tut-tutted about Moscow's temperatures, taking advantage of Aleksy's open account to empty her winter fashion collection into Clair's possession. After noting the wind-chill warning, Clair pulled on warm socks over the cuffs of her skinny jeans and layered a snug waffle print under a woolen turtleneck.

Her new faux fur boots were adorable as well as functional, their trim matching a smart leather jacket in the same buff tones. She topped it all with a corduroy baker boy hat and a pair of sunglasses worth more than her last pay packet. When she appeared, Aleksy said nothing, only shrugged into a thick ski jacket and laced up sturdy boots.

Clair paused inside the exit doors to check directions with the doorman. His English was excellent, but he stammered as he answered her questions, one eye on where Aleksy waited with detached patience. Clair took care to write down the street names phonetically so she could find her way back—exactly as she would have done if Aleksy weren't coming with her.

"Planning to ditch me?" he asked as they left the building.

"Of course not." Outside, the wind cut like a broadsword, making all her muscles contract and her breath stop in her lungs. She had to clench her teeth against them chattering. "Do you have a preference which way we go?"

"This is your walk."

Clair looked around her, determined not to let his attitude send her slinking back up to the flat. Taking a moment to get her bearings, she started toward the river, not stopping until they were overlooking the frozen water from a bridge twenty minutes later.

As she marveled at the jagged ice squares forming a broken path in front of the Kremlin, Aleksy withdrew a lip balm from his coat pocket and handed it to her.

So she wasn't *completely* prepared. Smoothing balm over her already drying lips, she thanked him and handed it back, getting a funny feeling in her center when she watched him use it too.

"You must be outside in winter often if you're ready for the weather," she said.

"It's still in my pocket from the last time I went skiing."

Oh. Of course. "Do you ski a lot?" Somehow she couldn't connect that detail to a man who was built like an athlete but didn't seem given to using his body outdoors when he could watch the financials from a treadmill.

"When I visit my resort, I do."

"Oh." Of *course.* "Is your ski hill here in Russia?"

"Canada. It's a heli operation. A good investment," he added.

"Of course," she murmured, smiling privately. Heaven forbid Aleksy simply buy something because he liked it. No doubt he thought *she* was a good investment.

That thought pinched enough that she wanted to get away from it. She began walking and he paced her, his formidable presence drawing startled looks, but ones of recognition. The average Russian citizen seemed to know him better than she did.

"What other sorts of enterprises am I keeping you from today? The internet said you got your start in road and rail transport."

He took a moment to absorb that she'd been cyber-stalking him, then answered, "Lumber first, then transport. Other types of manufacturing. Real estate of all kinds. A shipyard." He scowled.

"That one isn't such a good investment?" Clair guessed.

"No, it's very sound." His frown cleared to what looked like pride. "All of my ventures have excellent teams in charge."

"Then why the dismay?" she asked.

Aleksy was frowning because he couldn't think of one thing he was being "kept from" by this stylish blonde in her smart boots and cute hat. The way she was watching him so closely, trying to read his thoughts, was the exact reason he'd wanted to avoid her today. If her penetrating glances weren't bad enough, she was provoking yet more self-examination and he didn't like it.

"I'm thinking of what I would be doing in the office if I were there," he lied.

Her fine-boned jaw tensed, accepting the minor set down without comment as she looked away and walked on in silence.

He'd wanted to seal her lips against further questions, but he hadn't meant to hurt her. The truth was, he didn't know what he'd be doing at the office. His strategy had always been to set the personnel in place so a business ran itself, paying him dividends and allowing him to expand to the next challenge. Each new enterprise had been a step toward overtaking Van Eych, but there were no more steps. He'd reached the finish line. Time to put the game away. The work he'd put into amassing his assets suddenly seemed as pointless as tapping a plastic piece around a cardboard path. Yes, the wealth he'd accumulated would always need direction to keep him comfortable for the rest of his life, but it hadn't accomplished what it was meant to; he was still eaten by guilt.

And still confronting a gaping emptiness in his life that could never be filled.

A bright glint flicked in his periphery, dragging his attention over Clair's head to a man with a camera. He wasn't dressed for the weather and looked miserable. When Aleksy confronted him with a glare, he scurried off, not giving Aleksy the chance to turn Clair and say, *See? He was staked outside the penthouse and followed us.*

Disturbed, Aleksy followed the man with his eyes while he made a mental note to increase his personal security. The typical paparazzo didn't care if his target saw him. That kind of surveillance spoke of someone sniffing out skeletons in closets. A suffocating feeling rose like a band to close around his chest.

Clair's small hand suddenly gripped his down-stuffed sleeve, pouring buoyant lightness into the dark turmoil roiling inside him. Her wonder-struck expression made his heart lurch into a painful, stumbling gallop.

"When you said the streets were dangerous— Am I imagining things or is that a *bear?*" Clair tore her gaze from the astonishing sight down the block to catch Aleksy watching her with an expression of heartrending struggle on his face.

He turned his face quickly to look. By the time he looked back, the only emotion he expressed was sardonic humor. *"Maslenitsa."*

Clair's nerve endings were still vibrating as she searched for traces of what she had thought she'd seen in his eyes, but whatever had been there was gone. She ducked her head so she wouldn't give away how dejected his shift in mood made her.

Get a grip, she ordered herself, and released his arm, repeating the word he'd used. "What is it?"

"A festival to welcome Spring. Like Mardi Gras. Except we have bears, fistfights and troika rides."

"Judging by the first two, I imagine the third is bronco-busting a reindeer? And what makes you think spring has arrived?"

Aleksy chuckled, the rich sound so unexpected Clair had to swallow her heart back to where it belonged. He soon dispelled her misconception by securing them a ride in a sleigh pulled by three horses. Snuggling her into his side, he let the English-speaking driver tuck them under a blanket and educate her on the festival, which was pagan in origin, but also related to Lent. When Clair expressed too much interest in the bear wrestling contest, the old man turned in his seat. "Not for you, *malyutka*. Wrestling is for old men who only have vodka to keep them warm." He winked at Aleksy.

The man ended by fetching Clair a plate of *blini*, round pancakes covered in caviar, mushrooms, butter and sour cream.

"I can't eat all this. You'll have to buy me a whole new wardrobe," Clair protested after a few bites of the deliciously rich food. "Here. Please," she prompted Aleksy.

"No." He held up an adamant hand. "I can't eat pancakes."

"Too many as a child?" she teased, imagining him as a strapping boy gobbling everything in sight.

"Far too many," he said grimly. "If you can't eat it, give it to the dog."

She followed his nod to where a German shepherd was

licking a plate, the owner unconcerned. Clair let the dog wolf down what was left of her *blini* and disposed of the trash, her mind stuck on Aleksy's remark.

They moved under an ornately carved archway built of ice to a park filled with ice sculptures. The angels, castles and mythical creatures were beginning to thaw, their sharpest edges blurred, but they were still starkly beautiful, transparent and glinting in the sun.

"The driver said the festival has only been revived recently. You weren't eating pancakes just for Lent growing up, were you?" she mused aloud, stepping back and hiding behind her camera to keep the question less personal.

"No, we ate them for survival," he said flatly, gaze focused somewhere beyond the stunning sculptures.

"You weren't working for Grigori then?"

"I was hardly working at all. My mother wouldn't let me quit school."

Clair lowered her camera. "Somehow I can't imagine you taking orders from anyone, even your own mother."

"I would have given her anything," he said with a gruff thread of torture weaving through his tone. "I couldn't give her what she really wanted—my father's life back. I worked ahead and was in my last semester when Grigori hired me. My mother still worked at first, and at least we ate something besides pancakes. I gave her that much, at least, before she withered away."

His bitter self-recrimination caught her off guard, making her want to touch him again, but she was learning. He would talk a little, but only if they kept it to the facts.

"Cancer?" she guessed, unable to help being affected by his loss. He gave an abbreviated nod and she murmured, "That's tragic."

"It was suicide," he bit out. "She knew something was wrong and didn't seek treatment. I would have done *anything*—" His jaw bit into the word. "But she felt like a burden on me." His hand opened, empty and draped with futility before he shoved it into his pocket. "And she wanted to be with my father."

Clair caught a sharp breath, frozen with the need to offer him comfort, but very aware she couldn't reveal too much empathy right now.

"She must have loved him very much," she murmured, voice involuntarily husky.

"She was shattered by his death. Broken." His gaze fixed on a sculpture that had fallen over and splintered into a million pieces, its original form impossible to discern. "I hated seeing her like that. Hated knowing I—" He cut himself off and shuddered, looking around as though he'd just come back into himself. "Are you finished here?"

Clair huddled in the constricting layer of her jacket, aching for Aleksy even as she silently willed him to finish what he'd started to say, sensing he needed to exorcise a particularly cruel demon. Yes, she needed to keep from becoming too connected to him, but she couldn't ignore his terrible pain.

Carefully stowing her camera in her pocket, she put her hand on his arm. He stiffened against her touch, rejecting her attempt to get through to him.

"I'm sure you did what you could. Don't blame yourself for something you couldn't control," she said.

"Who else is there to blame?" he countered roughly, utter desolation in the gaze that struck hers like a mallet before he yanked it away.

A name popped into her head and she spoke it impulsively. "Victor?"

"Chto?" The word came out in a puff of condensed breath as he swung his head to glare at her.

"Did Victor—" It sounded stupid as she thought it

through, but she'd been keeping up with the headlines in London. Victor's perfidies were being revealed with glee by the press. Victims were pouring out of the woodwork day by day. Aleksy's hatred of the man was bone deep. His remark from last night, *"after my father was killed,"* still rang in her brain. Perhaps she was being melodramatic, but…?

"Did Victor have anything to do with how you lost your father?" she asked, tensing with dread as she tested this very dangerous ground.

A spasm of anguished emotions worked across his dark expression. There was grief and the reflexive hostility anyone showed when their deepest pain was exposed, but there were other things too. Frustration. Resolve. Remorse?

"It's not a connection I can prove," he said through lips that barely moved.

Her whole body felt plunged into an ice bath. To hear her vague suspicion met with such a condemning remark gave her goose bumps. He believed Victor had played a part in his father's death. No wonder he held her in such contempt for accepting generosity from a man with no right to the wealth he'd used to dazzle and persuade her. She felt sick for letting the advantages Victor offered outweigh a proper examination of the type of man he was.

Clair barely recalled the walk back, lost in absorbing the gravity of the injury Victor had dealt to Aleksy's family. No wonder Aleksy was such a hard, bitter man. The greater wonder was that he hadn't swept her onto the street the way he'd threatened to.

"Are you all right?" he asked when they entered the suite.

She looked up from removing her shoes, startled to see they were in the apartment. "F-Fine." Her lips were numb. "I think I need a warm bath." She could barely face him. "Walking might have been a bad idea after all."

His scarred cheek ticked in silent agreement.

Clair swallowed. "You can go into your office if you want. I won't go out again. I promise."

"You're still here."

Clair's bemused voice startled him, in a good way. She looked better. Her face was clean of makeup, her cheeks glowing from the heat of her bath. She wore yoga pants and a thickly woven pullover that hugged her bottom and clung to her thighs. Gorgeous.

He swallowed.

She'd been so wan after their morning out that he'd been worried about her, which unnerved him; he didn't normally feel more than superficial concern for anyone. She was turning him inside out.

"What do you have there?" he asked, trying to distract himself, rising with the intention of taking her load of laptop and files.

"I was going to work on the foundation in here, but if you'd rather I used the dining room—"

"No, here is fine." He looked at the cover of the laptop balanced on the stack of file folders as he set everything on the desk. The label jumped out at him with the company logo and its scrolled initials: *V.V.E.*

"It…was something he gave me to work on, then said I should keep it." She bit her lip, her upward glance culpable.

Aleksy tensed. The man was dead, but he just wouldn't *die*.

"I'll get rid of it," Clair said flatly. "I just want the foundation files off it. Then I'll throw it in the incinerator. Honestly, I feel so sick with myself!" She covered her cheeks with her hands, her blue eyes clouded with repentance. "I didn't realize he contributed to your father's death. You must be so disgusted with me for having anything to do with him. I am."

Mental walls were clashing into place, trying to lock out what she was saying, but the words were spoken. He couldn't ignore them. All he'd said earlier crept around him like coils of barbed wire, warning him any move would only tangle him up more painfully. He didn't know why he'd let himself delve back into his mother's grief or Victor's role in his father's death. He just wished he could forget them.

He suddenly stopped cold. What was he thinking? For twenty years those horrors had been uppermost in his life, driving him toward making Victor pay for them. To put any of it out of his mind was a betrayal of his parents' memory—but somehow the passionate hatred that had kept him going was now evaporating.

While Clair was seeping in.

His heart gave a hard, uncomfortable lurch—she was starting to mean too much to him.

She inhaled deeply, rousing him from his thoughts. He realized she was interpreting his expression and grim silence as confirmation that he did hold her in contempt. He scowled. "We met because of him. That's it," he tried.

"How can you say that when it's obvious you're angry and hate me for having anything to do with him?"

He was angry. Something was rising in him that he didn't even understand. Clair wasn't stupid, weak or avaricious. Why, then, had she let herself become involved with such a man?

"All right, yes," he ground out with enough fervor to make her start. "I want to know how, Clair. How could you let him near you? How could you not see him for what he was?" Unexpected, bile-green jealousy rose in him. "How could you—"

Not wait for me.

He jerked his head to the side, hands fisting defensively, terrified by what he'd almost said. His heart pounded and sweat broke on his brow and upper lip. He reminded himself that for all his possessive urges, he really had no right to her.

"In part, I was just very naive," she said with quiet self-reproach.

"I know you're naive," he countered, incensed by the reminder. Everything in him was programmed to protect that vulnerability in her, even from—*especially* from—himself. After all, if he'd finished his story earlier, he'd have revealed that *he* was ultimately responsible for his father's death. That his father had stepped into a fight Aleksy had started and that when Aleksy had finished it, he'd walked away with two lives on his conscience. Three if he counted his mother.

He kept looking for qualities in Clair that he disliked so he could feel less disgusted with himself for pressuring her into this arrangement, but she kept reinforcing that he was taking advantage of an innocent. Her next words proved it.

"It was the first time I'd been singled out as special. I was susceptible to that," Clair admitted in a small voice, eyebrows pulling together with humiliation.

Aleksy seemed to freeze into an even stiller statue. Clair experienced that old feeling of wanting to fade into the wallpaper, hiding her flaws so no one would see why she didn't deserve to be chosen and taken home. It was painful to stand tall and own her mistake. She clasped the edge of his desk, drawing strength from its solid weight.

"When I was growing up, the home had an arrangement with the school nearby. If we kept our noses clean, we could attend and have the same chance at scholarships and higher education as the rich kids. I gave it a shot, but I wasn't a genius, just average. And I wasn't rich. I always wore secondhand uniforms, never had trendy shoes, never got invited to parties. The kids weren't trying to be mean. I just wasn't one of them."

Aleksy's intense scrutiny nearly evaporated her voice. It was so hard to crack herself open and reveal this tainted, imperfect neediness inside her.

"When I got to London I wasn't special there either. I worked three jobs to make rent, so I didn't have time to date or party even if I'd wanted to. Then along came Victor. He treated me like I was the only one who could get things right. He needed me to be places for him and when I walked down the hall, people noticed me because they thought I was important." The last part tasted bitter. She'd known she wasn't important, but she'd liked that others had been deluded into thinking it. How pathetic.

Letting her hips rest on the edge of the desk, she gripped it with both hands, shoulders hunching as she spilled the rest. "He gave me things I'd never had, money for clothes. *New* clothes. He said he'd support the foundation."

"*I'm* doing that. Do *I* make you feel special?" His harsh voice grated over her exposed, sensitive core.

It sounded like a trick question. "I realize I'm just another mistress to you. I don't expect you to treat me as anything special," she said.

"You should," he shot back with startling vehemence. "You should expect every man alive to treat you as the smart, kind, remarkable woman you are. Do *not* sell yourself short and fall for scum like Victor." He rubbed his jaw so his final remark came out muffled and almost indiscernible. "Or me."

She took a moment to remind herself she'd only known him a few days, that he might know himself better than she did, but her urge to contradict him pushed her forward a few steps.

"Don't sink yourself into his class," she blurted, her hand going to his arm even though it was a risk of rebuff. "The way you make me feel—"

His arm was iron beneath her touch. She could feel his instant rejection, but his attention fixated on her mouth as though he was willing her to continue.

Clair had thought she'd been cleaved open to her very heart when talking about her secondhand upbringing. What she'd revealed so far was nothing, though, *nothing*, compared to confiding his effect on her.

Especially when he looked so severe, as if whatever she said would be refuted and thrown back at her. He was beautiful and dangerous, clad in black jeans and a black pullover that clung to hard pecs and biceps, someone who could squash her self-worth under a disparaging heel.

"I—" She had to clear her throat. Despite her terror at opening up, she was reacting to his closeness. Heat trickled into her fingers and toes, gathering in her loins. "The way you make me feel isn't some adolescent need for approval or status or…whatever I was looking for then. It's… good. I just feel so good when you touch me."

Her voice dried up and he was talking over her anyway. "Any man could make you feel like that."

She flashed him a galled glare and snatched her hand back. "I've never reacted to anyone the way I do to you."

Hurt started her pivoting away from him, but he snatched her back to face him.

"You haven't been with anyone else—"

"I haven't wanted to! That's the point. *You're* special. To me. To my body," she clarified. "I don't know why."

He blew out a frustrated breath. "It's the same for me. I don't understand it either."

"Really?" She shouldn't have asked. She should be more confident, not beg for confirmation that he liked to be with her, but she desperately needed to hear it.

He seemed to waver over what to say to that. She might as well have been naked, standing there waiting.

"You must know how you affect me."

She swallowed. His words arrowed sweetly into her heart, even though they only spoke of physical reaction.

"How would I?" she asked with a shrug that tried to hide her defenselessness. "You didn't want me to stay last night. You didn't want me to kiss you this morning."

His cheek ticked in the way she was beginning to know meant his own shell was being penetrated. "Kiss me anywhere," he said gruffly. "*Everywhere*. But not here." He touched his scar lightly.

Her heart lurched while her shield crumbled, leaving her unsteady and weak with longing.

"Do you mean that?"

His stared right at her. "What do you think?"

CHAPTER TEN

SHE BLINKED, TRYING to take in this new information, new freedom, to seek badly yearned for physical contact with another human. With him.

"Like…now?" she asked cautiously, feeling pulled toward him.

The air in her lungs felt sharp as knives. Desire and insecurity ground their rough edges together inside her at how easily he was lifting up her emotions and tossing them around.

He looked at her with the masculine arrogance he wore like a cloak, pure Aleksy, isolated and driven and powerful. She was only Clair, green, overwhelmed and too deeply enthralled by him for her own good. At least when he was the sexual aggressor she knew he desired her. To take up the onus of initiating lovemaking meant doing the unthinkable: asking him to want her.

But she really wanted him to want her. Really, really did.

"Every man enjoys being seduced." He shifted to lean his hips on the edge of the desk, contemplating her with a type of removed curiosity. "I'm no different."

Seduced. She'd meant a kiss, but she was reminded of the care he'd taken when she threw a similar challenge at him.

Acute inadequacy sliced through her at the same time, cutting all the sharper because the longing within it was so honest. She wanted their most intimate connection with all the pent-up hunger that never seemed to dissipate, but she wished she'd kept her mouth shut. Her base need for approval was too bone-deep, the risk too great if she failed to arouse him.

She shook her head and said with a papery laugh of bravado, "As if you'd ever give up control to anyone."

"You don't think you could make me?"

Her heart skipped, teased into hope by the light suggestion. "Could I?"

"Try," he dared.

He was all supreme confidence, and that intimidated her, but a flash of eagerness for the challenge surprised her, making her pulse leap and her nerves flutter. She didn't know what she was doing when they came together, each time so overwhelmed by his experience she lost all conscious thought, but the idea that she might be able to break past his wall of willpower excited her, making heat swirl and tingle into secretive places.

She tried to probe past his burned-gold eyes to the thoughts behind. Need was welling up to tight levels in her. She *wanted* to make him want her.

And he wasn't as detached as he wanted to appear. He was watching her every breath, waiting to see what she'd do.

That gave her the courage to take a few steps toward him, but as his heat and scent surrounded her, all her thoughts short-circuited. Her hands lifted instinctively, greedy to touch, but nerves arrested her.

He was so much bigger than her, his chest a wide plane bracketed by arms hanging with tense readiness, his biceps taut and straining against his pullover. She wanted to kiss his bare wrists, but imagined he'd think that inane.

His rib cage expanded as he inhaled, drawing her eyes to the lift of his strong shoulders, the tendons standing out with strain against his neck. He stared down at her from beneath his thick, spiky lashes, eyes flashing with frustration.

That revelation of want held firmly in check gave her the nerve to take the plunge. She moved to stand between his feet and set her hands on his shoulders.

He jolted a little, as if she'd burned him. She felt the leap of energy as an electrical charge, flaring awake all her senses. With the sort of smooth caution someone used when petting a wild animal, she relearned the familiar shape of his shoulders, hands warming as heat radiated off his muscles. She traced the ridge of his collarbone through the warm fabric of his shirt and when she reached his throat, she crept light fingers under his collar, circling until she found the bump at the top of his spine.

The hollow at the back of his neck was familiar territory. She stroked upward against the short spikes of hair on the back of his head. As she went up on tiptoe, she expected to feel his arms lock behind her, dragging her stretched body into his taut one. Then he would drop his head and kiss her. They'd be in the bedroom in seconds.

He didn't move, only looked at her.

Nobody will ever truly want you, Clair.

Her heart fell and continued to fall, like plunging into an icy crevasse, the descent long enough to comprehend what a mistake she'd made and dread the damage at the bottom. She felt stupid and incapable. A disappointment to herself and him.

Ducking her head, she eased her hold on him and lowered herself to flat feet, body unavoidably brushing his, making her almost cry with denial as she felt the bulge of—

Unnerved, almost fearful, she stared at where his jeans followed the contour of his hardness. Caught in a spell, she slowly reached out and traced the shape with a wary touch, then became aware of the searing affect she had. His breath hissed in and the shape of his erection grew pronounced, unmistakable.

She stared in astonishment. She'd barely touched him! The thrill that went through her nearly melted her onto the carpet at his feet. She wanted him, all of him, so badly. Her gaze skimmed over the wall of him again, starving eyes consuming a banquet. She didn't know where to start. Fear of revealing her extreme need paralyzed her. She didn't want him to see—

But maybe it was the same for him. Maybe it would excite him to know he was wanted, the way she'd just felt a rush of desire from recognizing his arousal.

It took all her nerve, but she lifted her face and let him see whatever was there. A blush of heated excitement, longing in her eyes, admiration for the sheer sexiness of the man he was. Licking her lips, she even told him, "I want to kiss you."

His nostrils flared as he drew in a sharp breath. Color flooded under his skin and his hands came up as though to grasp her hips. He caught himself and clasped the edge of the desk, knuckles white. With a jerk of his head, he acquiesced.

Clair used her hips to nudge his thighs farther apart so she stood right up against his erection. Her heart thundered. Aleksy lowered his head, but that was as far as he went. She had to press her mouth to his and cling to his shoulders for balance as she lifted herself on her toes. She had to open her lips and try to cajole him to do the same. His erection pressed insistently against her belly, but he didn't let go of the desk.

To her chagrin arousal grew in her despite being the one trying to arouse him. Touching him in any way made her body writhe with desire while the taste and feel of his smooth lips against hers clouded her mind. She wanted to lose herself in the kiss. She wanted this to be the kind of all-encompassing kiss he always gave her.

He wasn't cooperating, though. His breathing was erratic, but he didn't seem as overcome as she was. Growing frustrated, she cupped his head and boldly forced her tongue into his mouth.

He grunted and leaned into her. Surprised by her success, she tried again and was met by a welcoming draw and the stroke of his tongue against hers. Now came the drowning pool of pleasure where she ceased thinking about the mechanics of what they were doing and hummed with gratification at the sheer joyfulness of kissing him. Nipping, soothing, consuming. Arching her body, she stroked herself against him, ready to abandon herself completely.

His hard fingers dug into her hips and he straightened away.

She whimpered at the loss and licked her lips where the taste of him still lingered.

"Aren't you going to move this to the bedroom?" he growled.

The fire building inside her was doused, leaving burning hot embers that blistered her sensitive nature. She had thought his innate drive to lead was ready to take over. He was determined to make her work for this, though, and it almost undermined her belief in herself and what she was able to make him feel.

Trying to understand where she had gone wrong, she searched his expression and noted the tension in his face, the tick in his cheek that made his scar pull at the corner of his slightly parted mouth. His chest was expanding in a short hard rhythm.

In a startling burst of clarity she knew why he'd stopped

her. The kiss had started to become more than he could handle. He was cooling the pace so he could remain in control.

A heady sense of power flowed into her, but it was surprisingly tender too. With renewed confidence, she reached out and learned how to open a man's jeans.

"I don't have a condom in here," he warned.

"You don't need one."

Aleksy swore in Russian. Stop her, he told himself. Before she put him over the edge. But he was too hungry to see how far she'd go. The rush of blood in his ears deafened him and the heat of desire threatened to spontaneously combust his soul.

He reached for the soft swells teasingly rising and falling behind a thin layer of wool. She often went braless. He loved it. Those modest, taut breasts of hers didn't need support and he liked being able to find her nipples easily and feel them harden.

Clair stepped back, her light grip catching his thick wrists before he'd barely cradled her soft curves. "No touching. Not yet," she said breathily. She pressed his hands back to the surface of his desk. "You'll distract me and I want to make this as good for you as you always do for me."

Anticipation screamed in him, threatening to make him lose it completely. He instinctively wanted to take over, be the one in control of the pace, especially when her hot blue gaze clashed into his, her enjoyment of having the upper hand obvious.

"I want to suck your nipples," he demanded, balancing on the knife's edge between stealing the dominant role that was always his and letting Clair keep the power she was obviously reveling in.

He almost had her. Her pupils expanded into galactic holes he could have fallen into. Her breath rushed out in a near surrender and her light hands on his thighs grew heavy as she melted closer.

"No," she gasped at the last second, the word driving like a knife into his groin. She dug her fingernails through denim as she firmed her resolve. "Not yet. I want to take off your shirt first."

With hands that betrayed a nervous tremble, she tugged the close-fitting knit up his chest. He lifted his arms, eyes closing as he endured what felt like the loss of his skin. Her lips touched his collarbone.

He caught back a groan.

Another kiss and her splayed hands smoothed across his chest hair. His nipples went so tight they felt pierced. His erection pulsed in the space of his open fly, clawing at his control.

Her hands began to graze with more surety, flowing over his rib cage and abdomen, finding his waistband. Working with awkward inexperience—which was its own delight—she eased her hands under denim, lifting his hips off the edge of the desk to work his jeans down his thighs.

"Finally," he hissed, shaking with need.

She paused and he realized he'd spoken in Russian. She kept going and he kicked out of the jeans, stepping so his socked feet were braced, fingers flexing with desire to catch her up to him and plunder her mouth.

She lowered herself to her knees, hands cool and soft on his calves as she removed his socks. Did she know she was driving him to the absolute edge of reason?

He glared down to see her staying on her knees, gaze coming to rest on his shorts, lips pressed into a line of uncertain study. As she reached out and carefully eased the elastic over him, his vision blurred. He stepped out of his shorts and didn't know if he'd be able to stay on his feet. He was a conqueror by nature and necessity, but at this second he was a slave. A prisoner to each of her incremental movements.

Despite knowing what she was about to do, he was staggered by the first touch of her hands, swelling and hardening to unbearable proportions, filling her palms. Words of protest and abject begging threatened to burst from him, but she was stealing every last thought from him, closing her mouth upon him with untutored, scandalously sexy ardor.

A ragged groan erupted from him. His passion nearly exploded. He wasn't going to last and he wanted, *needed*, to be inside her.

With the very last shreds of his control, he tangled his fingers in the golden silk that brushed her cheeks. It killed him to force her to release him, but he had nothing left. He was about to shock or scare her and he had to have her with him when the last of his restraint evaporated. He wanted to feel each ripple of her orgasm when he came and know she was as insanely lost to pleasure as he was.

"You didn't like it?" she asked anxiously as he drew her to her feet.

"If you don't get a condom on me soon, you're going to have to start arousing me all over again." He couldn't believe the quiet, husked voice was his own. He sounded tender. He even felt a deep, complex stirring inside himself. To say, "I want you" didn't come near to encompassing the expansive need in him.

The phrase still caused her blue eyes to glitter with jubilation. That naked look nearly made him use the desk right there and then.

He cupped her head so he could swoop his mouth onto hers and did everything in his power to convey his desire, to bestow as much pleasure as he could. Her sweet moan, the plaster of her lithe body into his, was his reward.

Swinging her into a cradle against his chest, he made the bedroom in record time, barely able to open the drawer for a condom and get it on without erupting. He removed her yoga pants and the panties beneath with a rending of delicate lace while she pushed off her top, her breasts hot and damp with sweat as he pressed himself over her, crushing her onto the bed beneath him. Using his knees to push her thighs apart, he couldn't resist testing her arousal, finding her so wet and ready she bucked at the first touch of his fingers.

In one triumphant thrust, he filled her. A primal tingling raced down his spine as he made her his, only his, again and again and again.

CHAPTER ELEVEN

ALEKSY TOLD HIMSELF he was allowing the relationship to continue, and deepen, for Clair's sake. Of all the men she'd come across in her life, she found him to be sexually compatible, so he was putting himself at her service. It would be unkind to deprive her of an opportunity to explore her sensual nature. At least he knew she was unique and treated her accordingly. Some might call it self-servicing, but he disagreed. No one had ever gone out of their way to make her happy. She deserved to be spoiled in every way, so he was doing it.

It wasn't his usual exchange of luxuries for sex either. They were both getting exactly what they wanted from that side of things.

His mind drifted to the other morning when his housekeeper had called in sick. Clair had made him breakfast. As her short robe had fluttered around her bare thighs, teasing him with glimpses of her bottom, he'd grown so hard his appetite for food had fallen to a distant second behind his hunger for her. She'd noticed.

Seated on a kitchen chair, he'd pulled her to straddle him and they'd teased and tantalized each other, playing out the lovemaking, holding back even when he was inside her, driving each other crazy until he'd had to knock his eggs to the floor and take her on the table, urged to thrust hard and fast by her breathy pleas. They'd climaxed together, vocal and near violent, and had been equally shaken and quiet afterward.

He'd taken her back to bed, where she'd slept against him, her head a kitten weight on his chest. He had dozed, but mostly he'd berated himself for failing to use a condom.

What was he trying to do, tie her to him forever?

He hadn't brought himself to mention it when she had stretched awake against him, but later in the day she'd shyly informed him she didn't think pregnancy was an issue and that they'd have to curtail their favorite activity for a few days.

A weight of disappointment had settled on him, one he'd blamed on abstinence, but they'd been back to basics this morning and even though he was still fogged with sexual satisfaction, he was also aware of a cloud of unease hanging over him.

Guilt.

The more he learned about Clair, the more he knew how badly he'd taken advantage of her. If he had the least shred of conscience in him, he'd give her up, but watching her natural reserve evaporate was positively entrancing. She had made the first move this morning, rolling atop him and telling him how much she'd missed making love with him. How could any man be expected to forgo waking up to that?

Unable to bring the ends of this particular rope together, he stopped gazing out the window and gave up pretending that he was working. His ambition was nonexistent. He'd only been in the office an hour, but he began to pack up for lunch, excited as a schoolboy for the ring of the bell. Lazlo had inadvertently revealed while arranging Clair's credit card the other day that her birthday was coming up. She had become flustered and dismissive when Aleksy had asked her how she wanted to celebrate, eventually confessing that birthdays had always been a disappointment along with Christmas.

He was determined to turn that around for her, starting with a visit to the city's best jeweler on his way to meet her at an exclusive, sky-high restaurant. Enjoying the way she reacted when he surprised her with toys and trinkets didn't make him selfish, he told himself. It was the opposite.

Wasn't it?

A short time later, however, as he scanned past diamond rings to bracelets and pendants, he recalled the way his father had often taken pains to barter for some treasure or another that his mother had coveted. Once it had been a sewing machine, another time a pair of gold earrings. His father had rubbed his hands in glee at being able to surprise his wife with her heart's desire.

That's all he, Aleksy, wanted to do for Clair, but it felt as if he was making false promises. The sparkling rings mocked him. He couldn't keep this up, keep *her*, forever, even if he wanted to.

Did he want to?

He clenched a fist, aware of a deep need to have her as readily at hand as everything else that was vital to his existence. Air, water. Clair.

Shaken, he dismissed his misgivings and set down a small fortune on a choker with sapphires in graduated shades of blue, brilliant and sparkling as her eyes when she laughed. He *liked* seeing her happy. Provoking her to smile didn't make him a bad person.

His certainty lasted through a pleasant lunch where she practiced her fledgling Russian phrases and he expanded on some of the historical events she'd been reading about. She made him look at his city and country with new eyes, and hers widened with dazzlement when she unwrapped his gift.

"It's too much," she protested in a whisper, then teared up as her cake arrived, topped with half a dozen sparklers. "Aleksy!" Her lips trembled and she threw her arms around his neck, hugging him hard.

The most incredible tenderness infused him as he pulled her into his lap, startled by how much emotion he'd drawn out of her with such a little act.

"Your secret is out now, you know," she said in a strained voice, drawing back enough to swipe under her eyes and offer him a beaming smile.

His heart did a sharp dip and rock in his chest. "Which secret is that?"

"You're the biggest softie in the world. Not nearly as ominous and gruff as you want to appear."

His mouth twitched and his conscience gave him a kick. He was misrepresenting himself if she really believed that.

"Can we keep it between us?" he said lightly, not wanting to spoil the mood, but pressing her back into her own chair.

"Of course," she replied with an enigmatic smile. "I like knowing more about you than anyone else does."

The remark niggled at him as they finished their coffee and left. His security had told more than one parked car to shove off over the last month, but there hadn't been any for two or three days. His real secret was still safe.

Nevertheless, he was so distracted by his inner thoughts as they walked out of the building that they were in the scrum of paparazzi before he realized he was their object, not one of the international celebrities also dining here.

The clamor and flash and jostle was bad enough, especially with Clair to protect. He squeezed her to his side, aware of her hardening into a tight ball as the horrific questions were shouted not just in Russian, but English.

"Aleksy! Are you guilty of murder?"

* * *

After Aleksy's remark about the paparazzi noting whom he'd taken to the Bolshoi, Clair had made a point of searching their names online each day. Sometimes she noticed a photographer aiming a lens at them as they stepped out, but not always. The gossip hunters were sly and determined, however. Every outing was documented whether she was aware it was happening or not, including their impulsive appearance at the *Maslenitsa* festival.

Being stalked unknowingly made her queasy, but until this circus, her main worry had been the helplessly enamored expression on her face that matched the one worn by his previous lovers. So much for her detachment!

But how could she be impassive when he'd made himself into her own personal playground? Each time they came together she grew a little more possessive of the territory she conquered. Now he'd gone out of his way to do something special for her, buying her a ridiculously extravagant gift and—even more precious—revealing a kind of thoughtfulness that made her feel maybe, just maybe, they were forming a connection that went beyond physical.

Still glowing with a sense of being exceptional in his eyes, she let him carry her along to the sidewalk, where they were suddenly mobbed in a way that truly frightened her. Ducking from the chaos into Aleksy's solid presence, she tried to make sense of why this was happening and *what were they saying?*

She realized she understood more than the Russian moniker of *Scarface*, but other names. Victor Van Eych. His son.

"Did you know about the private investigation?"

"How do you respond to the accusation you sent Van Eych to an early grave?"

"You've been arrested for murder before. Are you guilty?"

The words smashed through her euphoria like a rock through a window.

Seconds later, Clair found herself shoved into the back of his town car, jolted by more than the sudden end to the snapping and snarling of the paparazzi frenzy. Aleksy gave Ivan sharp instructions to return them home as he jerked loose his tie and ran fingers into his hair, then made a call in Russian.

She stared at him, conscience squirming at what was going on in her mind, but she couldn't help the reaction. That white line on his face seemed too revealing.

Murder?

His cheek ticked. He knew what she was thinking and his face hardened, but she couldn't help how shaken she was. Adrenaline saturated her blood. She tried to scramble herself together, tried to stop trembling, but she kept asking herself, What kind of man had she attached herself to?

One who bought her a necklace she somehow still had gripped in her tense hands. Also a new laptop, new smart phone, a tablet. Clothes, meals, tickets to shows. There was no end to the generosity he bestowed on her, but he wasn't really soft and kind. He was hard and angry if she cared to remember their first meeting and—her mind tripped to think of it—capable of murder?

No, her heart cried, but his expression wasn't that of someone who was incensed at being falsely accused. There was too much resentment. Too much bitter resignation.

"We'll go to Piter," he said once they'd made it into the safety of his flat. When she only stared blankly, he clarified, "St. Petersburg. Things will be ugly here for a while."

Uglier than right now? He was like ancient iron, all pitted darkness with grim angles in his face. Her mind was grappling to process the impossible. One question burned on her tongue: *Is it true?* Her heart pounded.

"We?" Her lips felt numb.

"You're not going back to London if that's what you're thinking." Implacable.

She gave a near-hysterical choke that wasn't anything like a laugh. "I don't know what I'm thinking." Her gaze circled wildly, searching for a place to land, glancing off the illusion of a home she'd begun to see in these flawlessly decorated walls.

If she hadn't been with him outside and heard those shouts, would he have told her the reason they were leaving Moscow? Or would he be selling this sudden trip as a romantic getaway?

Would she have bought in? Was she that naive and desperate for affection?

"Pack for staying in." Acrid hostility coated each word.

She swallowed, ears ringing. She'd never felt so alone in her life, so aware that her complete disappearance would go unnoticed by the world.

"I need to know what happened, Aleksy." Her stomach trembled, but she managed to keep her voice steady as she met his forbidding gaze.

"I told you that some people will do anything for money." A vilified sneer pulled at his lips.

"Like lie?" *Please tell me it's all lies.*

He stared at her, his gaze not the hard, sharp, dangerous blade she expected. It was supreme blankness. Bleakness. Flat, unpolished bronze.

"Of course lie, but in this case it was a betrayal of official duty, exposing a truth that should have remained buried."

His words knocked the wind out of her. She had to consciously force herself to draw a breath. It seared her throat and made her chest ache. Her skin grew clammy and her stomach tied itself into knots. She had one thought. *Go.*

As she looked past him, gauging her chances, his arm shot out, not touching her, but making clear he wouldn't let her leave. "You're coming with me, Clair. Whether you like it or not."

Everything in her gathered for the fight of her life. Before she could do more than engage his stare in a battle of wills, he ground out, "You have nowhere to hide and they'll eat you alive. I won't let that happen. But I won't touch you either," he added bitterly.

His statement was another shock, so oddly protective when her head was screaming at her that he was a danger to her. For some reason, her stupid brain stumbled on that *I won't touch you* as if it were a trip wire that sent her metaphorically splatting onto her face, pride bruised. She should be relieved, but she just felt rejected. *Again.*

Words crowded her mouth, but her throat was too thick to voice any of them.

"I have security posted at all the doors to keep the paparazzi out." He stepped back. "They'll also keep you in, so you might as well give in. I really don't need the extra humiliation of carrying you kicking and screaming to the helicopter."

He walked away to his room, presumably to pack, leaving his words repeating in her head. *Extra humiliation.* As if *she* were in a position to injure *him*. Cause further injury even, because he was already hurting.

Was he hurting? She rubbed where her breastbone felt as if it were coated in acid. For a long time she stood in the lounge, arms wrapped tight around herself, confused. Frightened, but not by Aleksy. By herself.

She wanted to trust a man who'd just confessed to murder.

CHAPTER TWELVE

CLAIR HAD HEARD Russians talk about their *dachas*. She had gathered they were a type of summer cottage retreat, usually rustic and far enough out of the city to offer a garden plot and a return to nature. The buildings were often little more than shacks, but they were kept in families for generations.

If this was Aleksy's *dacha*, he needed to work on his definition of *shack*. The minute she saw it, her mind heard, *Welcome home.*

They'd flown over nothing but trees once they'd left the outskirts of Moscow, leaving little to distract from her inner turmoil until she'd glimpsed a palace surrounded by a groomed park. The fountains were off, the canals frozen, but she'd realized they were nearing St. Petersburg. This was a place so beautiful even czars chose to summer here.

Far from summer now, the day was overcast, late afternoon flakes beginning to fall. The fresh dust of snow only made the expansive estate they touched down on look fresh and new. Untouched.

It was very new, she realized, looking at the bare, young fruit trees and nut groves that embraced the charming house. The two-story structure was built along old-fashioned lines with a wraparound porch, shuttered windows, pretty gables and a romantic turret. It was big enough to host a crowd, yet cozy and inviting. Not threatening and not something she would have expected Aleksy to build or buy.

As the pilot prepared to lift into the forbidding sky, stirring up a cloud of powdered ice, Aleksy reached onto a porch beam. "The agent said—here." He showed her the key, then opened the door, pressing her inside before the man-made storm hit.

The interior smelled of paint, freshly cut wood and newly laid woolen carpet. All the surfaces gleamed. It was tastefully decorated in masculine colors, spacious and unfussy like its owner, but welcoming.

It struck her as a fresh start. A promising one.

Clair swallowed, reminding herself why she was here and who she was with, but choice and logic had been left back in Moscow where the apartment building had been surrounded by long-lens cameras. She really would rather take her chances with this lone wolf than the pack of coyotes baying at those doors.

And this house felt safe, drawing her in despite her misgivings. The main floor made a circle from front parlor to the dining room, passing a staircase that climbed to an inviting landing. Upstairs, a quaint powder room with a jetted tub overlooked what might be a stream if spring ever did arrive. The bedrooms with their gabled windows begged for cradles and rocking horses and train sets.

Did Aleksy harbor fantasies of a family? she wondered with a clench in her chest.

She silently followed him as he inspected everything, pausing at the threshold to the master bedroom, taking in the huge space and vaulted ceiling from the door.

He noticed her hesitation but covered his reaction with an impassive assessment of the enormous bed, the dark blue coverlet and the walk-in closet. She supposed an equally spacious en suite existed beyond the door on the interior wall.

"What do you think?" he asked.

She thought she was in love but didn't think it would be judicious to say so. "It's beautiful. You've never seen it? Is it yours?" she added as it occurred to her this could be leased as a bolt-hole.

"It is." Aleksy searched for signs of approval in her, not sure why it was important to him. The house was only a thing, and he was past believing the acquisition of things ruled Clair, but he couldn't deny that he wanted her to like his home.

He'd settle for her liking his things since there was no chance she'd feel anything toward *him* except repulsion.

Gut-wrenching loss threatened to breach the walls he'd used to brace himself when she had demanded answers at the penthouse. He'd known his past would come between them eventually, whether he revealed it or not. It was the reason they had no future, but he would have preferred they had separated naturally, before she knew any of this. It broke something in him to see her view of him damaged. To see her fear him.

The woman who'd lately been greeting him with shy smiles and the warmth of her touch now held him off with a white face and mistrust in her eyes. He cringed and looked away.

"Did you design it?" she asked, yanking him back to reality.

"To some extent." Aleksy shrugged out of his jacket and tossed it on the bed. Fantasies of her white-blond hair and peach-flushed skin against the sea of blue tantalized him, but he ruthlessly shut them down. He'd promised not to touch her.

Keeping his voice without inflection, he explained, "My father worked in logging camps when my parents were first married. The accommodations were drafty bungalows. My mother never complained, but when my father was able to buy into a mill and make his own lumber, he built her a proper house. I used that floor plan as a starting point."

Clair cocked her head, her whimsical smile sad enough to puncture the heart he'd hardened to get through this. "You always surprise me when you're sentimental."

"Sentimental?" The word arrested him. He suddenly saw the monument for what it was. He'd told himself he was building a place to go to, anticipating time to relax once he defeated Van Eych, but it turned out this was yet another attempt to resurrect the dead.

"I thought I just lacked imagination," he dismissed, hiding his perturbation by circling a finger in the air, urging her to turn so he could help her out of her coat.

She huddled deeper into the thick folds for a moment, long enough for questions to flash into his mind like so many charges off one fuse. Armor against him? Didn't want him too close? Didn't want to risk his touch? Wanted to be ready to run when he stopped watching her long enough?

With a skittishness she hadn't shown since that first day, she offered him her back.

As he stepped behind her, she tensed and cleared her throat but only said, "It's not a lack of imagination to surround yourself with the familiar."

Her scent clouded around him, so evocative of their closest moments his abdomen tightened. Heat poured into his loins. He ruthlessly controlled himself and drew her coat off her shoulders, focusing on the inane conversation to dispel the sexual awareness overwhelming him.

"Trying to fix the past by using what's left in the present is foolish."

"Don't call it foolish!" She spun. Her hair whipped his knuckles in delicious castigation.

He inhaled and she folded her fingers into fists that she tucked under her bent elbows.

"The trinkets I have of my parents' could have belonged to anyone," she charged quietly. "They don't offer the kind of memories that would let me pay this kind of homage. Your parents loved each other and you cherish that. There's nothing foolish about building that into your home. I'd give anything to have a house built on love."

She really knew how to skewer a man. How did he explain that he'd taken the love in that house and personally caused its loss? He clenched his teeth so hard his jaw ached.

"This was a stupid idea," he muttered in Russian, wondering how he'd imagined they'd be "safe" here. He brushed past her. "I'll get the luggage in and start a fire."

Clair could have walked away. She was half sure Aleksy wouldn't stop her. Bundled for the weather, passport and credit card secreted in her pocket, she even got as far as trudging into the snow off the front porch.

The world was still and quiet. The low clouds had pulled back from the horizon enough to let a glimmer of dying sunlight slant across the pristine blanket that surrounded the house. Instead of forging a path to the road, she was drawn into a bower of trees where the bare branches hung around her like silver-shot lace.

As she absorbed the sight, she conjured a picture of her own face with darker hair behind the curtain. Her own voice said, *Come out, love. Daddy's home.*

In the time it took her gasp to condense on the air and disintegrate, the memory was gone.

Clair brushed at where snow drifted down and left tickling paths on her cheeks, eyes closed now, listening to her own jagged breaths as she tried to decide if it had been real. Why now? What did it mean?

Nothing, of course. It was fanciful imaginings brought on by talk of nostalgia and childhood. She still longed to run inside and tell Aleksy she had remembered her mother.

Oh, she ought to run from him, never mind the fading light and long walk in the cold! *But why?* He'd never once hurt her. Not on purpose. Maybe he'd said some things that were a little too blunt and honest, but he was always conscious of his strength around her. If he found the least little bruise from their intense lovemaking, he berated himself and kissed it better. He wasn't going to turn into some maniac who wanted to harm her.

In fact, what he'd turned into was a man who'd ejected himself from her bed before she'd had to refuse him. His personal code of honor had forced him to. That action didn't fit against one of the most dishonorable things a person could do, and it made her want answers, not escape.

Penetrated by the cold, Clair picked her way back to the house, stepping in her own footprints so she wouldn't further mar the immaculate field of snow. She walked around to the back of the porch, stamping her feet and then sweeping the snow away before stepping into the kitchen rubbing her arms and shuddering.

Aleksy stood pouring vodka into a short glass. He knocked it back before saying, "Finished making snow angels?" through his teeth.

"Are you drunk?" Her equilibrium was yanked by that unexpected twist.

"Russians don't get drunk." He poured another one, then stoppered the bottle and stowed it in the freezer. "They get tough." He moved, loose but steady, to where a tin of cocoa sat on the bench. He spooned some into a cup and poured steaming water from the kettle. Before he handed it to her, he tipped half the contents of his vodka into it. "Warm up. You're not used to this kind of cold."

Clair cautiously put away her boots and hung her coat. The hot mug of cocoa filled her cupped hands with warmth. She let the steam rise to scald her frozen nose.

"Are you hungry?" he asked. "I can make soup."

"Maybe later," she said, faintly bemused at this domesticated side he was revealing. Not exactly the "tough" he was referring to.

He leaned on the refrigerator, staring so hard at her she should have smoldered and caught fire. "I watched you out there, waiting to see if you would run. You looked about twelve with the snow past your knees."

Clair felt twelve again, sinking into a miasma of confusion, hormones flashing like dysfunctional neon lights, the weight of adult emotions threatening to overwhelm her.

"I just wanted to stretch my legs," she lied.

He snorted, swirling the clear liquid in his glass. "There was a time when I took for granted the girls who walked in front of my house. More than one did before I had whiskers and a scar."

"You want me to believe females haven't been falling on your doorstep all your life, scar or no scar?" She forgot about the vodka in her drink until she sipped and it bit back. Heat slid through her all the way to her toenails.

"The young girls were different," he mused into his glass. "They were like you, the kind who knew they wanted to marry and have a family."

"I don't know that," she said, flat but strong, eyes immediately seeking a place to hide. "I might have believed it when I was twelve, but it's not something I still fantasize about." That felt like lying again. She sipped her cocoa, savoring the glowing warmth that spread outward from her midsection. "Too many lessons in remaining realistic," she added, recalling all those childish hopes and adolescent crushes that had amounted to nothing.

Aleksy winced. "You told me not to be ashamed of being sentimental. Don't be ashamed of wanting those things, Clair. I did. Then. I imagined I'd choose one of those girls after I'd made my fortune."

"Were you in love with one of them?" Her heart stilled.

"No," he scoffed, and her knees unaccountably sagged. "But I was arrogant enough to enjoy the idea of them falling in love with me. I was convinced I'd have my pick when the time came."

Clair frowned, hating that word. Pick your teams. Picked last. Never picked.

Skipping over it, she asked, "What made you stop wanting that? Your mother's grief?"

Empathy stole over her like a fuzzy veil, partly due to the vodka slipping into her bloodstream. It made her feel tender, hurting for him when she considered how painful it must have been to witness his mother's heartbreak over the loss of her husband. At least he was there to see it and not locked up in jail….

Clair frowned into her cup, thinking the booze was a bad idea. She was having trouble clicking together important pieces of the puzzle.

Aleksy wasn't speaking, only staring into his glass, face lined with anguish.

She watched him, his powerful shoulders crushed by a weight. He looked…lonely. Inconsolable. She ached to circle his waist with her arms and press her face into the warmth of his chest.

"Aleksy," she began.

"Yes, seeing my mother's pain killed whatever illusions I had of leading that kind of life. Especially since I caused her grief and destroyed the happy life she'd finally been given." The words were dragged out of him and left on the floor like internal organs.

"Finally?" she repeated tentatively. Apprehensively. "Wasn't she always happy with your father?"

"Of course," he conceded with a shrug, "but they struggled for years. Everyone in Russia did. When my father organized the cooperative that bought the mill, it was a chance for a future, but still just a chance. They worked hard for every potato we ate. I should have said she finally had *hope*."

He drew a long breath, seeming to steel himself. His voice hardened.

"The problem was, profiteers were moving into Russia at the same time. One tried to bribe my father into selling his controlling interest in the mill. He refused and we were harassed for months."

Clair closed her eyes as dread stole through her. "Victor."

"He gave the orders. Lazlo has uncovered more evidence and will make it public soon. Victor's son knows what's coming and was trying to discredit me by revealing my past, but the attention will turn back on him once the truth about his father's actions come out. I don't think you'll be bothered too much after that," he concluded without emotion.

When he sent her back to London, she gathered with a little shiver. She was just getting used to sharing her life, and it was almost over. Her feet hurt and she realized she was scrunching them, trying to dig into this place, not ready to be uprooted.

"What exactly did Victor do?" she asked, afraid to hear the extent of it but needing to know before he sent her away. "Did he steal your father's shares? Take the mill?"

"A man came to our house and set it alight in the middle of the night."

Clair gasped and covered her mouth. The house like this one that she adored? "While you and your parents *slept?*" Horror gripped her. "And your father—?"

"Ran outside behind my mother and me. The arsonist was still there. My father told me not to go after him, but I had had enough. I didn't see the knife until he did this." His hand lifted to his face, his expression twisted with old fury and fresh pain.

"Oh, Aleksy," Clair breathed, terrified for him. Everything in her wanted to rush forward in comfort, but he radiated too much pain, as though the least thing would break him. "And you were just a teenager." The pieces were falling together quickly now, forming a tragic, unbearable picture.

He shuddered.

"A boy's temper in a man's body. I would have been killed if my father hadn't intervened. He lost his life saving mine." He slugged the vodka and set down the empty glass with a sharp *clunk*. Then he looked at his hand. His voice seemed to come from far off. "I don't remember doing it, but it's in the statements to police that I killed the other man."

"I can't believe they arrested you!"

"Why wouldn't they? A crime had been committed." He turned to the freezer to retrieve the bottle. "It was ruled self-defense and, supposedly, sealed because of my age."

Ever-deepening levels of dreadfulness rippled over her. A deliberately set fire. A narrow escape. Petrifying violence. Catastrophic loss. His life nearly taken. She never would have known him. The thought pushed tears into her eyes.

And all at the hands of a man she had trusted and relied on. Bile and self-disgust rose to the back of her throat.

Aleksy would *never* pick her. Not to live with him forever. Her awful connection to Victor would always be between them.

"I'm so sorry," she said with remorse, wishing the words weren't so inadequate. "I had no idea Victor could do something so vile." She took a deep swallow of the cocoa, seeking the numbing effect of the alcohol. The sweetness made her gag. She set it away, revolted.

"What about what *I've* done?" A scowl of self-hatred ravaged his expression. "I'm no better than the paid assassin who killed my father."

"You were fighting for your life!"

"I shouldn't have fought at all. I got my father killed and destroyed my mother."

She shook her head. This was why he isolated himself. He thought he was some kind of monster. "You can't punish yourself for a…mistake."

"A mistake that lasts forever."

"If you let it," she asserted. "You can't blame yourself, Aleksy. Victor brought about the tragedy by starting it, not you."

"Stop it." He stepped forward, every muscle bulging in confrontation. "I saw how you looked at me when you realized what I'd done. I know what you really think of me."

"No," she cried, assailed by guilt. "I was in shock from something completely unexpected. I didn't know what to believe—"

"How could it be unexpected? It's right here!" he railed, pointing at his scar. "From the first moment anyone sees me, they know what kind of man I am. You should have run far and fast the first day we met."

"You didn't give me a chance, did you?" she shot back, angry at his rebuke.

"No," he agreed with a bitter bark of laughter. "No, I didn't, but that's the kind of man I am." Snatching up bottle and glass, he elbowed his way out of the kitchen into the lounge.

CHAPTER THIRTEEN

"I'M NOT RUNNING now, am I?" Clair challenged behind him, barreling through the door on his heels.

Aleksy halted, teeth clenching as he searched for patience. Did she not realize his control was hanging by a thread? Without turning back to her, he guessed harshly, "Because you don't know where to go? Call Lazlo. He'll arrange a car and hotel."

"I'm not afraid of you, Aleksy Dmitriev!"

Funny, he was terrified of her. Setting down the bottle and glass with deliberation, he turned and said, "You should be."

"Why? Are you going to hurt me? Kill me?"

He jerked his face to the side, blind to all but splashes of color in his field of vision while he dealt with the sense of being rent open. No, he could never harm her, but he couldn't have her poking heedlessly into his old wounds either.

"Back off, Clair."

"You're not a monster, Aleksy," she said more gently. "You're generous and compassionate and honorable."

"What are you trying to do? Make it okay in your head that you ever let me touch you? I took a virgin for a mistress. I bought you clothes and gave you money for your charity because *I wanted to have sex with you.*"

Her breath caught as if she'd taken a stiletto to the lung. "That's not true," she gasped. "It wasn't just sex. Was it?"

He mentally stripped her fleece vest, insulating V-neck and loose jeans, imagining her naked skin catching the glow off the fire, her nipples pulled into dark, shiny points by his mouth, her thighs relaxing open under his hand. "Very good sex," he ground out, dying because he'd never have her like that again.

"Then why are you trying to take a bottle to bed instead of me?" she goaded, angry hurt pouring a wild flush into her cheeks. She had the gall to charge close enough to stand toe to toe with him, breath chocolate-sweet and as innocent-smelling as the rest of her. "You could be sugarcoating your past and trying to seduce me right now. You know you don't have to try very hard, so why don't you?"

His skin tightened and her upper arms were in his flexing hands before he could stop himself. Her slender muscles always shot a warning through him. *Take care.* The protective instinct couldn't be overridden even when he was feeling so threatened he wanted to shake the daylights out of her.

"Don't think I won't give it a shot," he growled. "I'm not in a frame of mind to stop either."

She only dared him with a tiny hitch of her chin.

He searched for vestiges of fear in her expression but wound up homing in on her lips. A tiny shudder quaked through her as temptation crackled in the air.

The weight of his head weakened his neck. "Stop me," he ordered dimly, speaking against the damp, ripe plum of her mouth.

He almost had her. She almost said it. He felt her begin to shape the word, sensed her tongue tucking behind her teeth. If she'd said *no*, for any reason, he would have made himself stop.

Her eyes fluttered closed and she pressed her open mouth to his.

She smelled of snow and chocolate and vodka, sweet and hot. And he was *hurting*. His deepest shame was never meant to be on display like this. He felt flayed to pieces by today's revelations. By her reaction. But when he drew her into him, the pain subsided. The tattered edges of his soul came together and began to mend.

She moaned softly, igniting him. With one step, he had her back against the wall, her neck and the curve of her hip filling his hands, her delicate softness cushioning all his hard angles. Her fingers wove into his hair, pulling him into a kiss he couldn't have ended if the house had fallen down around them. Her tongue stroked his, her throat straining as she reached for the same oblivion he was in. With a growl, he fumbled the fly of her jeans, pushing them down, lifting her as she kicked free and bracing her against the wall so she could lace her legs around him. He needed to be inside her. Needed her.

As he tried to free himself, her fists clenched in his hair, pulling his scalp tight as she dragged him back from the kiss enough to gasp, "Condom?"

It wasn't *no*, but it made him hesitate. He distantly put together that he was about to risk a pregnancy. He couldn't put a baby in her. Him, with his tainted soul.

The deepest agony filled him as he carefully pushed her legs off him and supported her until she stood. Confusion broke through her flush of arousal. "What's wrong?"

"Leave me alone, Clair." He walked outside where the gathering darkness, frozen and harsh, matched what was inside him.

* * *

His rejection devastated her, but, Clair realized, she'd hurt him first.

The knowledge stunned her, hovering like a dark cloud as she took a long bath and tried to sleep. She'd always been the one hurt, always taking it to heart when she was overlooked or misjudged or found wanting. To her knowledge she'd never delivered anything but mild disappointment when she declined a date. The fact that she'd penetrated Aleksy's hard shell was as shocking to her as how deeply she'd stabbed him behind it.

She stared into the dark, her mind unable to stop replaying those few minutes in Moscow when she'd learned about his past. *I saw how you looked. I know what you think of me.* She had let him down when he'd already been feeling humiliated by the uncovering of his deepest pain before the entire world.

Maybe she should have read more into his scar from the very beginning, but even though he was formidable and ruthless, she'd only ever seen that blaze as an injury, never a warning of cruelty or aggression. She'd instinctively understood it was the result of deep pain.

And maybe if they had more going on than sex between them, she might have had more immediate trust! She was nothing to him but his latest mistress, though. He'd made *that* clear while she was performing her little exercise in proving he had honor.

And she had certainly failed to think that through! She clenched her eyes shut, still throbbing with heat between her thighs while the rest of her ached with wounded disappointment and fear. Had honor stopped him or did he not want her anymore? He'd seemed as excited as she was, only stopping because she'd reminded him about birth control. She'd said it because she couldn't bear to trap him into something he didn't want. If they ever married, she wanted—

Clair sat up, instantly shaky and clammy all over. Where had that thought come from? She didn't want to marry anyone.

Did she?

Yes! She curled into a ball, trying to contain the longing that exploded in her like a supernova. Years of denial were blown into fragments as, within seconds, a brilliant future unfolded in her mind: her with Aleksy and children in this house full of affection and laughter and love.

She was falling in love with him and it made knowing he only felt desire—maybe not even that anymore—unbearable. Her mind shot back to Paris and his, *I'm not the marrying kind*. She yearned to believe that was just the self-inflicted punishment he'd hinted at in the kitchen tonight, but even if it was, there was no guarantee he'd ever be interested in marrying *her*. Every solicitous, tender moment he'd shown her had been a prelude to sex. Because he wanted her body, not her. Never her.

With an angry sob, she threw herself back onto the pillows, ordering her longing back into its box, but it was futile. The fantasies continued.

Eventually she quit tossing and turning, sleeping hard from her journey through such taxing emotions and waking to a brilliant day. Coffee was already made when she entered the kitchen and Aleksy's boots and jacket were missing. A quick glance out the window and she spotted him shoveling the snow off the drive.

When he wasn't in his office over the next few days, talking and talking in every language he knew, that's where he was, outside in the cold. She tried to stay busy preparing the final details for the launch of Brighter Days, but Aleksy filled her mind. Every time she saw him, he looked exhausted, as though he was barely sleeping. The media demands were obviously getting to him. She only wished there was something she could do, but he didn't seem to want to share—which was one more layer on the cake of hurt she was carrying inside her chest.

Clair wasn't sure how much longer she could take it. Then her mobile rang unexpectedly. It was Lazlo.

Startled to hear him identify himself, she asked the only sensible question that could explain his ringing her number. "Are you looking for Aleksy? He's upstairs. I was just going to ask him what he'd like for lunch."

"Please don't disturb him. He's doing a live Web conference off his laptop. No, I'm calling for you, Ms. Daniels. I want to discuss the press release on your contribution to our investigation."

"I haven't contributed anything," she broke in.

A significant pause; then, "As it happens, the calendar details you kept of Victor Van Eych's appointments proved very helpful."

"Oh." Clair turned to sit on the stairs.

"We'll be stating that even though you had no knowledge of the misappropriation of investor funds, it was thought you could be in danger from associates who might have feared that you did. This is why, despite any appearances otherwise, you have been the platonic guest of Aleksy Dmitriev since the takeover."

Clair was glad she was sitting. Her blood seemed to drain out of her head, leaving her feeling empty as everything vital in her slithered away.

"Ms. Daniels?" Lazlo's voice came from a long way away.

"Yes, I'm here. Is that what we're stating?" she said, straining not to sound shrill.

"It neutralizes speculation and affords you more privacy in the future."

"When I'm on my own, you mean."

"Exactly," he said without hesitation. "Please respond to any questions or requests for interviews that you aren't at liberty to divulge anything until it has all gone through the courts."

Clair doubled forward, glad she could hear the rumble of Aleksy's voice behind closed doors and knew he wasn't likely to see her like this.

"When do I leave?" she asked tightly.

"To return to London? After the interview today, the worst of the media storm should be over. Everything is in place for when you're ready."

By "everything" she supposed he meant a flat, a job and fifty thousand pounds. Blood returned to her cheeks with hot pressure, sharp with the sting of degradation. Of not even being Aleksy's *mistress* anymore.

"Ms. Daniels? Did you have a comment?"

"None," she choked.

"A perfect response."

CHAPTER FOURTEEN

ALEKSY EMERGED FROM his office with a hole in his belly and an even deeper hunger to see Clair. Her quiet, thoughtful nature had been his salvation through this week of scrutiny, painful questions and trial by public opinion. Each time his mind had been drained of his last wit and his defenses battered to nothing, she'd rescued him by simply being here with fresh-baked cookies, humming to old rock tunes or napping in front of the fire.

He'd offered to bring someone in to cook and clean, but Clair had said she didn't mind doing it and he'd been grateful. He didn't want anyone around. He'd been prepared to send her away, had requested Lazlo to put everything in place for her return to London. He'd thought he wanted to be alone to lick his wounds, but since he didn't have to hide anything from Clair—

That thought brought him up short halfway into the kitchen.

Clair knew his worst secret and she was still here. Through the course of this week, everyone else's reaction had ceased to matter because this one woman, in her tough little way, had skipped the platitudes and supported him with her steady, warm presence in his home.

His soul, locked in a paroxysm of agony for so long, began to unbend, sighing at the release, burning with the return of feeling. It made him wince as he looked at the table set for two. Another stunning realization struck: he was taking her for granted.

"What's wrong?" she asked, turning to catch his scowl.

"Nothing." He shook off his dismay, thinking, *I might ask you the same.*

Clair's hair was loose and she was doing her best to hide behind it as she fussed with putting out salad and hot sandwiches. The little he could see of her face was pale, her lip caught between her teeth, her tension visible in the way she moved.

"You must be bored stiff, locked away like this," he surmised. "Would you like to go into the city for dinner?"

It was an impulsive offer, something he didn't think through, and it surprised her. A sleek decorative bottle full of oil and vinegar dropped from her hand, shattering on the tiled floor. Clair muttered a word her prim lips didn't usually form.

"Stand back," he said, noting her socked feet. "I'll do it."

A few minutes later they sat down to eat. She'd mixed fresh dressing into a measuring cup but was still out of sorts. "I liked that bottle," she groused.

"It can be replaced, Clair." He didn't understand why that made her jaw set and her eyes grow bright. "Look, I appreciate all you've done this week," he tried. "When I brought you here, it wasn't with the intention you'd housekeep for me. I just wanted you out of the line of fire."

She stared for a moment, thoughts contained behind her slightly flushed cheeks and sober expression. "Throwing your jeans into the laundry with mine wasn't exactly a strain. How is…everything?"

Yet again he appreciated the way she took care to probe gently. Many times she'd let him get by with a grumbled

"Fine." He had the strongest urge to lean across, brush her hair back from her cheeks and kiss her.

He hadn't touched her since that first evening when he'd almost taken her in the lounge. In truth, he hadn't trusted himself. His emotions had been all over the place and he'd still been hurting from her initial reaction and angry with her later one. He had needed to shove the entire world away while he dealt with old pain and the lurid interest in his past.

Now he was overwhelmed with a sense of indebtedness along with a desire to be close to one person: Clair. As close as physically possible. He wanted to make love to her, tenderly and thoroughly.

"You don't have to talk about it if you don't want," she said, dabbing a fingertip onto a fallen sesame seed and touching it to her tongue.

Her words snapped him back to the kitchen, but his libido remained transfixed on the action of her tongue, the press of her lips, the faltering curiosity in her gaze as she looked at him.

He didn't disguise the heat rising in him. When she saw it, a flush of desire blossomed on her cheeks, but her eyebrows came together in confusion. She skittered her gaze away and held herself still, not rejecting him, but not screaming with receptiveness either.

Sweat broke out on his brow.

In the space of a few minutes, he'd convinced himself that she'd merely been waiting for him to warm up to her again. She was here, wasn't she? But he hadn't given her much choice in the matter. *At any time*, as she'd ferociously pointed out the other day. Would she even have become his mistress without his high-pressure tactics?

His center of surety, slowly coming back online after this horrific week, backslid a notch. With aggressive determination he leapt to thoughts of how he might continue buying her affections, but that route was distasteful now. He pushed a frustrated hand through his hair, answering her because he didn't know what else to do.

"Today was the worst, but it was my last word on the subject. The result doesn't look like it will be as bad as I feared." He supposed a part of him had expected police to knock on his door to take him away in handcuffs again, but it was all in the past. Just a story that had needed to be repeated until a different story drew interest.

Her expression softened. "You thought you'd be vilified, but two decades of proving yourself as a man of principles couldn't be completely discounted, could it?" she challenged quietly.

He felt cornered by her words. She kept trying to frame him as good and honorable when he had always known he was bad and needing to repent. That was why he didn't cheat or steal, but even at that, he had resorted to bribery with her, hadn't he? He was sitting here plotting how to coerce her to stay in his bed.

Shame pinned his gaze to the food she'd prepared for him. "You're imbuing me with a much higher character than I possess."

"Aleksy, don't. You're a good man. You deserve to be happy. If you cut yourself off from the life you once thought you'd lead, you're letting Victor win."

So earnest. So blind. So determined to turn him into something admirable.

Some of his hopelessness must have shown in his face, because she blurted, "I'm not trying to persuade you into anything, not with me. I'm just saying you shouldn't write off a meaningful relationship because you think you gave up the right."

Not with me.

"What about you?" He felt his blood slowing with time. "Because you deserve to be happy too."

"I know." She swallowed, blinking rapidly, head down. "I've had a lot of time to think since I've been here."

Aleksy didn't understand why her saying that staggered him. He'd already figured out what kind of woman she was. He'd chosen to believe her when she said otherwise, but he'd known. She'd been a virgin. A powerless one that he'd exploited. He was utterly sincere in telling her she deserved everything that her heart desired.

It would come at a terrible cost to him, but he'd pay it. For once, he'd act with the sort of honor she thought he possessed.

Clair held on to her composure with superhuman effort, losing hope as Aleksy's expression grew stonier, washing away the footings of her confidence. She reacted by pulling herself inward, taking refuge behind an air of insouciance that wouldn't betray how much this really meant to her.

"I wasn't lying when I said I wasn't looking for a permanent relationship. When I was a child, all I ever wanted was to be adopted into a family." She set down her fork and folded her hands in her lap, aware of him becoming still, listening so closely the air around them seemed to vibrate. "As the years passed and I wasn't chosen, I convinced myself being part of a family was the last thing I wanted. I really believed it. Self-preservation, I suppose." She shrugged, the movement jerky and not nearly as careless as she wanted to be.

His slow blink was almost a wince.

Clair could hear the voices in her head warning this gamble wouldn't pay off. It made her keep a few cards against her chest, only saying, "But living in this house, thinking about how your parents felt about each other and, I believe, how my parents felt, as well… It made me realize I want a different kind of family. Not parents, but a husband and children."

Her clammy fingers had clenched themselves together under the table and she kept them hidden, fingernails digging into the backs of her hands so she wouldn't betray how anxious she was for him to show some sign he wanted those things too. With her…

"I understand." He sat back, his mouth curling with self-deprecation. "I knew you weren't proper mistress material— Clair, that's a compliment," he hurried to say when she gasped and stood, impaled by the remark.

She began clearing the food they hadn't touched. "No, you're right," she rushed out, clattering dishes. "I know I'm not good at this." She was breaking into pieces on the inside but refused to let him see it. It would only make this worse. "When we met, I was afraid of every type of relationship. I was so terrified I'd get hurt, I didn't let anyone near me. Now I know it doesn't actually kill you to be close to someone. Literally, physically close, I mean." Her smile was brittle. "I'll be able to take that forward…"

She stumbled to a halt, unnerved by the way his eyes went black. Jealousy?

Ducking her head, she let her hair fall forward, hiding her confusion. Hiding the way her face wanted to crumple because she was so full of longing and so unsure.

With a deep breath, she steeled herself and lifted her chin. "Still a long way off before I risk falling in love, but…" She trailed off, bravado tank on empty. "I'm just sorry I'm not—" Her throat began to thicken. *What you wanted.* "I'm going to pack."

She rattled dishes onto the bench and left.

CHAPTER FIFTEEN

IF ALEKSY'S WORK ethic had suffered when Clair was waiting at the penthouse for him, it downright evaporated when she wasn't there at all. He told himself that sinking into new challenges would allow him to leave this gut-knotting anguish behind, but nothing seemed to bury it. He didn't really care about the outcome as his legal counsel cut a deal with a union to keep a factory operating and when a stock market correction dented his worldly holdings. His only concern was whether it had affected the portfolio he'd put together for Clair.

He went through the motions of living, but nothing drove him. He'd never been at such a loss. Genuine hunger, guilt, thirst for revenge… They'd all motivated him to face the next challenge and the next, and now he had no goal. No purpose. The only thing that meant anything to him now was gone.

Clair.

He'd done the right thing, he kept telling himself. She deserved to be loved. He, at least, had known the feeling at one point in his life. He'd subverted his need for it, determined to avenge the lives of his parents, but they'd made sure he knew what it was. Clair hadn't experienced that, and if she could find a man who loved her even half as much as he did—

The thought flashed through his mind like lightning, and then a million others crowded in a rumble behind it.

He loved Clair. He loved her with the kind of devotion that would move him between her and a knife or a gun. He would die for her.

A second jolt of stunned clarity went through him. That's what his father had done. He'd only ever seen his father's death as something he'd caused, but his father had stepped into the fight because he'd loved his son too much *not* to protect him.

No other man would ever love Clair as much as he did.

Did that make him worthy of her? No. But as it sank through him that he hadn't even told her how deeply she was loved, he felt like the smallest man on earth. Her husky "Not with me" continued to ring in his ears all day, every day, but maybe if she'd known how thoroughly she occupied his heart, she would have felt differently. If nothing else, surely she'd realize her own worth and never again settle for anything but wholehearted devotion in a relationship.

Stirred from apathy for the first time in weeks, he sought out her new contact details.

And quickly learned she'd disappeared.

Clair made a note in her calendar, then traced the capped end of the pen over her upper lip, pleased with the number of "yes" responses she'd had to her invitation.

The home usually had a decent turnout for volunteer drives. Clair was one of the diehards. She had expected a few of the people she'd seen during the annual clean to be willing to sit on her committee bridging the foundation funds to the most-needed programs in the home, but she was thrilled to hear all of them eagerly agree.

Things were finally coming together. The home had

cleared out an old cloakroom to make an office for her. One of the cooks had offered Clair the use of her mother's house while the woman visited relatives in Australia. Clair only had to feed the cat and pay the utilities. She wasn't taking a wage from Brighter Days, but she'd interviewed for a clerk position with a notary in the village. It was only a temporary maternity cover, but it would keep her on her feet until she figured out her next step.

She was, if not happy, at least comfortable and rewarded while she nursed a rejected heart from Aleksy's virtually wordless goodbye. He'd driven her into St. Petersburg himself and put her on a private jet back to London, where she'd been met by that dead fish, Lazlo.

She shouldn't be so hard on the man. Lazlo was only doing his job, being attentive to the point of smothering her, ensuring that her boxes had been delivered to the flat in one of the most exclusive buildings in London. *Aleksy's?* She hadn't had the nerve to ask. She hadn't lowered herself to take any of the three jobs he'd secured for her either. As for the credit cards that bore her name but wouldn't send their bills to her, she'd cut them up the minute Lazlo left.

Clair knew it was pigheaded, but she hadn't stayed one night in London. She'd put her things back in storage at her own expense and caught the train here. A clean break, she had decided, smirking a little over using the expression. Look at her, proficient in the vernacular of modern-day relationships after her first one.

Sighing, she flipped the page on her diary to check the time on tomorrow's appointment with an art therapist before she closed the book. This was the part of the day she found hardest—going back to a house that felt like a home and having only a cat for company. Perhaps she'd invite one of the staff and their family to eat with her. She did that now. Rather than forcing herself to tough out the lonely times, she was making real friendships and finding it a confidence booster. It turned out people liked her when she opened up and let them get to know her. She wasn't an awkward orphan any longer. She was an independent young woman like any other.

Fetching her jacket off the hook in the corner, she shrugged it on, flipping her hair out from under the collar with a vague thought to trim it soon. Outside, she noted a stylish car in the drive. Her heart skipped a beat, betraying how many fantasies she still harbored about a certain man, but it was probably just the school trustee who'd promised to pick up the scholarship information Clair had left for her.

Hearing a footstep and a creak of a floorboard behind her, Clair said, "Is that you, Geri? I was just about to hunt you down and ask if you'd like to come for din—" She turned to see a tall shadow filling the doorway. Déjà vu struck instantly.

She couldn't move as she took in tall, dark, scarred, gorgeous Aleksy Dmitriev invading her life again.

"Who is Geri? Is he your colleague?" *That voice*. His rough-smooth accent and deep timbre vibrated through her, making her feel restless and anxious to take flight.

Clair surreptitiously braced a hand on the windowsill behind her. "Geraldine is one of the house parents. What are you doing here?"

"You dropped off the face of the earth, Clair." He stepped into the tiny room and she took in all of him from his uncreased suit to his smoothly shaven jaw. He looked restored to his old self. Better. Like clay that was stronger for going through the fire. Clean, polished and strong. "What were you thinking, disappearing like that?"

Given that her mind was a clean whiteboard at the moment, completely blank of anything but shock, she took a moment to shake herself into a response.

"I wasn't trying to disappear. I only wanted to discuss the foundation with the people it would most closely affect, so I came here to do it. Why?" She didn't like how he put her on the defensive. He'd set her out of his life like bottles for the milkman to collect. She didn't have to answer to him.

At least, she wanted to be that defiant and dismissive, but in reality, her heart was caving in on itself and her entire being was soaking up the effect of being near him again.

"If you didn't want to stay in London, you should have said." His arrogant decree was stated with a scowl of impatience.

"Said to who? Lazlo? Nothing against the man, but he's not my warden and definitely not my bosom chum. He already knows more about my private life than I ever wanted him to. I wasn't about to report my comings and goings to him."

"To *me*." Aleksy loosened his tie, then drove his fists into his pockets, his agitation making her think for a second—

Clair gave her head a little shake, refusing to read in to it. She had let herself get all tangled up in wanting things from him and was still trying to unravel him from her heart. She didn't hate him for hurting her, but she didn't want him to do it again.

Even though she suspected he *was* doing it again and all he'd had to do was step through a door.

"We're no longer involved," she said with as steady a voice as she could muster, reminding herself as much as him. With a flick of her wrist, she prompted him to close the door. When it had clicked firmly and he turned the blinding brilliance of his bronze eyes back on her, she countered it brutally. "You paid me out, in case you didn't know."

His jaw hardened. He leaned into the door, chest rising

as he absorbed her offense. "I'd promised I would. What else would I do? Renege?"

"You didn't have to do all that other stuff." She folded her arms, unable to look directly at him while she relived the sting of being bought off for her sexual favors. She had thought they had shared their bodies with each other freely. Hers had definitely been offered without expectation of compensation.

"I'd promised you that too."

"Well, I didn't have to accept it, so I didn't," she spat out with rancor, hating how cheap he'd made her feel.

"You still could have told me where you were going," he bit out. His voice was so censorious it made her stiffen. "You didn't have to disappear without a word. An email doesn't take any effort at all."

Taken aback by that, Clair choked out a laugh. "Oh, didn't you get my response to yours?"

His eyebrows slammed together. "I didn't email you."

Clair only lifted her eyebrows, waiting for the penny to drop.

With a muttered curse, Aleksy pushed his hand through his hair and tried to pace across the tiny space of her office. He only moved two short steps before swinging back to her.

Clair snapped to attention, aching from the tension of holding herself in this state of readiness. Her palms were sweating within the knots of her fists. "Why are you here, Aleksy?" It seemed rather cruel, quite honestly. She'd managed to move on with her life, not well, but she was doing it. This was going to be a setback of epic proportions. There would be fresh tears she didn't want to shed.

"I'm here to find you." He said it impatiently, as if she ought to know. "I didn't know where else to look, so I came here to ask if they had any contact information on you and they told me you were down the hall. I almost had a heart attack."

Intensity radiated off him, as though he was still keyed up from the discovery.

"There's such a thing as a telephone. You could have called the office," she pointed out. Heat rose on her cheeks and she shifted. The room was too small to contain them both. "Why didn't you put Lazlo on the job? He probably tagged my ear with a GPS when I wasn't looking."

"I was worried." He seemed uncomfortable with the admission, but the words came out of him as though they wouldn't stay inside. "You can't just walk away like that, Clair," he scolded. "I've lost people I loved, and that pain doesn't ever go away. Not knowing where you were or if you were safe was equally as bad."

All her defensive anger fell away, leaving a heart that began beating wildly. She reminded herself that he was just a very protective man with a ferocious sense of responsibility. This wasn't personal.

"Aleksy, I grew up here. Right here." She pointed to the ceiling where two floors up she had shared an attic bedroom with a number of different girls over the years. "To get a workspace in this building, where wards of the state live, I had to pass about a million background checks. That's how serious they are about security. I'm living next door to the police chief. The bus driver greets me by name and his wife sells me eggs. Where do you want me to live that you think I'd be safer?"

He had his unmarked cheek to her and she saw how utterly beautiful he would have been if both sides of his face matched. When he swung his face around, she was almost relieved to see the scar. It made him human and reachable. Mortal.

His jaw worked as though he wanted to say something

but thought better of it. A long minute of silence drew out, pulling her nerves taut.

"You're happy, then?" he finally asked, cheek ticking.

She hugged her coat around her as she shrugged. "It's a little like I've come home, even though..." She frowned, searching for the words. "I feel good because I know I'll make positive changes for the children here, but it's still a place that makes me sad. I wish..." She had to press her lips together to keep them from quivering. "I wish they all had proper homes to go to."

He nodded and the empathy in his expression was more than she could bear. A lump lodged in her chest and she looked away.

After a moment, she found a wry smile even though it was the last thing she felt like doing. "I'm not used to checking in with anyone, you know that. I should have at least told Lazlo not to pay the rent on an empty flat. Sorry about that."

"The money doesn't matter." Aleksy seemed to consume her with his eyes. He'd accomplished his goal, so she wondered why he didn't leave. She was safe here, but the longer he lingered, the more danger she felt. She ached to touch him. Give herself over to him. Again.

Sucking in a breath, he asked a question that shocked her. "Are you seeing anyone?"

"A *man?* No!"

Aleksy's chuckle rasped her nerves. "Why do you say it like that?"

"Because—" Clair's heart clenched. She felt her eyebrows pull together in a pained frown and turned to the windowsill to hide it, tracing some long ago child's initials carved into the wood. She couldn't find her voice to continue.

"You told me that's what you wanted." He sounded confused.

"I did. I do! I'm just not ready yet." She wasn't over *him* yet.

He didn't say anything. She found the courage to glance back at him and found him eating her alive with his eyes, a tortured expression on his face.

He still desired her. It made her insides quiver with yearning. She felt the same way. Pulled.

"Aleksy, don't," she pleaded softly, increasing his agitation.

"I know, I know. *Not with me.*" He grimaced.

The bottom dropped out of Clair's world. She wasn't sure if she understood. "Aleksy," she said haltingly, his name like honey on her tongue, "I thought you understood… Oh, I wish I could make you *believe* that you're as entitled to happiness as anyone. Why do you have to say that? 'Not with me.'"

"*You* said that," he countered harshly.

"When?" But even as she said it, she remembered and closed her eyes.

"That last day in the kitchen," he growled. "You went off about how I should subscribe to the Happy Ever After channel, but *not with me*."

"Why on earth would I say *with* me when I'd just gotten off the phone with Lazlo and knew you were already sending me away?" she cried, aghast at how her voice cracked, revealing the stunning pain that still reverberated through her when she recalled it. "You didn't even want me as a mistress anymore."

She clenched her teeth, throat scraped raw as she thought of how she'd laid it on the table as plain as she'd been able. He'd stared at her with that same impenetrable stoniness he turned on her now.

"You spoke to Lazlo that morning?"

She jerked her shoulder. "He called me. To tell me that

you were downplaying our relationship in the press," she added in a charge. "Not even wanting to acknowledge we ever had anything between us—" She kneaded the place between her eyebrows, making her eyes sting.

"Clair, I was doing everything I could think of to protect you. Giving you an easy way out. You know what my life was like then."

"No, actually, I don't," she railed, lifting her glossy eyes to him, vision too blurred to see the way his expression contracted with pain. "You barely told me anything. Never looked to me for comfort or… You hardly looked at me at all!" She snatched up a tissue with a shaking hand, mortified she was falling apart like this. "Not that we had that sort of relationship," she reminded herself. "But I would have listened. I was trying to be there—"

"You were." He was suddenly close, far too close, big warm hands covering hers as she tried to dab at her eyes. "You have no idea what it meant to me that you were there. The only bright spot I had. Don't cry. Don't let me make you cry. I can't bear it."

She was shaking even worse, swimming in the scent of his aftershave. His heat and strength reached out to her, making her want to sway into him and hold on tight.

She swallowed, trying to brush away the solicitous hands wiping the tears off her cheeks. "Don't."

"Don't what?" He cradled her damp cheeks in his firm palms, making her entire body tremble. "Don't try to protect you from every possible thing that could hurt you, including myself?"

"Is that why you sent me back to London?" she asked, stretching to understand what had seemed impossibly cruel and was far beyond what she could accept as reality.

"You wanted to go, Clair. I'd already forced you into

an affair you didn't want. I couldn't keep you when you said you wanted to go."

"You didn't force me."

"Don't say that." He dropped his hands and took a step back. "I showed all the finesse of a Neanderthal, conking you in your tender heart for this place, threatening your reputation, practically throwing you over my shoulder to carry you to my cave."

"You really are your own worst critic. I know how to dial the police if I need them. I wouldn't have gone with you if I didn't want to."

"You really are naive," he countered with a feral glint in his eyes that made her pulse skip. The way he sobered and watched her so closely made her heart beat even faster. "Did you want to go when you left Russia?"

The question backed her into a corner. Her feet tingled with a need to retreat while hot-cold shivers raced over her. She crushed the damp tissue she still held, knuckles going white.

"Please don't ask me to be your mistress again," she managed to say.

"I won't."

The backs of her eyes filled with a hot sting. What a stupid thing to ask, she berated herself.

"Don't," he groaned, and suddenly she was yanked against his chest, off balance and caged by hard arms that held her in a gentle grip when she reacted and began to struggle. "Listen, Clair. Please listen for just one minute," he whispered against her hair.

The movement of his lips on her skin stilled her more than the words, plucking at her heartstrings as she recalled all the tender ways he'd touched her. Need stirred in her, liquid heat settling low, preparing her for the pleasure they gave each other.

"You came into my life when I thought I had only one thing to offer a woman. I made you my mistress because that's all I was capable of. I couldn't offer myself. I was a shell. A robot programmed for revenge. And you were the last woman I should have had anything to do with. I didn't even understand why I had to have you, I just did."

"It was a temporary need for human closeness. I understand. I felt the same." She pressed for escape.

"No! That's not what it was. You were like the sun coming back after the longest Arctic winter. I was bitter and frozen and suddenly I was thawing. Feeling. Do you know how much it hurts when feeling starts to come back into a numb limb?" His fingers wove into her hair and stroked the nape of her neck.

"Oh, Aleksy," she murmured, hating to hear of his suffering. Drawing back, she reached to cup her hand against his scarred cheek, feeling the muscles tense beneath her touch. She almost pulled away, but he covered her hand and closed his eyes. Turning his mouth into her palm, he pressed a kiss into her hand before letting her touch settle against the jagged line again.

"Are you really able to accept all that this scar means?" he asked with a mixture of anguish and hope.

"It means you're a man who would fight to protect the people he loves. That's not something to be ashamed of."

"I am. That's what I came here to tell you. I would die protecting you."

His image blurred as her eyes filled with tears, afraid to believe what she was hearing.

He moved his hands over her with fervent possession. She couldn't seem to catch her breath, especially when he looked at her with uncertainty edging the blaze in his eyes.

"Can you imagine for a minute how difficult it has been for me to know that you deserve every type of happiness and be completely convinced I'm the last man who can give it to you?"

"About the same as it feels for me?" she suggested, feeling something crazy and optimistic battering at the thinning shell she'd always held tightly around her heart.

He shook his head. "All you had to do was stay and I would have been the happiest man alive."

The feeling inside her became massive, too big to be contained. "How could I stay when you didn't seem to w—" Her chin crumpled and she bit her bottom lip, vision blurring again.

When she would have drawn back, he hugged her close, his thickly accented words breaking her open. "I want you, Clair. Of course I want you. I love you with all my heart."

She shuddered at the cataclysm of hearing him say that, at feeling love all around her as he held her tightly and pressed hot kisses to her wet face. Her hands sought to grasp all of him, sliding up his chest, over his flexing shoulders, following the line of his tense neck, smoothing over his hair.... Their mouths met in damp, sweet, poignant ecstasy. Clair's heart was so full it was going to explode.

In a move of agile, male strength, he hitched her to sit on her desk, sending files skating to the floor. Bracing his hands next to her hips and his forehead sternly against hers, he said, "Tell me you're not just reacting to the first man to tell you that. I don't have it in me to be noble and give you up again, Clair. A man like me loves for life, and this is it."

Life. She smoothed his bottom lip with the pad of her trembling fingertip. "Just because I'd never had sex before doesn't mean I didn't know what it was or ache deep down to experience it. It's the same with love. I don't need a hundred men to compare to in order to be sure what I feel for you is the real thing."

"Good, because you're not getting a hundred. You're not even getting one other man," he muttered with a self-deprecating curl of his lip. He tilted her chin up, his gaze so tender it warmed her to her soul. "Are you too shy to say it properly?"

She smiled, stunned by how easily the words formed on her tongue. "I love you."

The expansive emotion seemed to fill the room. The adoring smile he gave her as he stroked her cheek made fresh tears spring to her eyes, happy ones. His kiss was reverent and full of longing.

"Aleksy," she said, reluctantly breaking a kiss that so easily could have spun into something very compromising. "This is my work. There are children here. We have to take this off-site if we're going to keep this up."

He sobered. "Can you leave? In the long term, I mean. Can you—will you—work from Russia or must you stay here? We can come back whenever you're needed," he promised.

She melted, thrilled but at the same time incredibly touched by his understanding. "Thank you for seeing how important the foundation is to me."

His ironic expression made her chuckle.

"I didn't sleep with you *just* for the foundation," she insisted.

"I'll choose to believe that," he said with disgruntlement. "But you'll marry me for no other reason than that you want to."

Not a question. A demand. Wounded he might be, but never weak. Her grin widened. "Of course I will. But I'm given to understand I have to anyway. A woman's virginity belongs to her husband, doesn't it?"

He didn't betray one iota of compunction, only smiled with wolfish satisfaction. "True. But I don't just miss you in my bed," he added with deep sincerity. "I miss you in my life." With utmost tenderness, he asked, "I mean it, Clair—will you come home with me? Be my wife and make a family with me?"

All the details flitting through her mind scattered, completely eclipsed by the momentous wish that had just come true for her. She couldn't even speak she was so overcome.

Aleksy tensed as a shadow passed across Clair's face, but when he tilted up her chin, her blue eyes gleamed. Her joy was so tangible he could taste it like spun sugar on his tongue.

"I always wanted someone to come here and say that to me," she managed to husk. "It was worth the wait."

Aleksy's heart expanded beyond what he could contain. Pressing his mouth to her crooked, trembling smile, he drew her into his arms.

"No more waiting. I'm here now."

* * * * *